APPALACHIAN RUNAWAY

*A Dog's Tale
for Grown-Ups*

Rachael Roberts Bliss

Jan-Carol
Publishing, Inc
"every story needs a book"

Appalachian Runaway: A Dog's Tale for Grown-Ups
Rachael Roberts Bliss
Published January 2025
Little Creek Books
Imprint of Jan-Carol Publishing, Inc.
All rights reserved
Copyright © 2025 Rachael Roberts Bliss

ISBN: 978-1-962561-60-0
Library of Congress Control Number: 2025930417

You may contact the publisher:
Jan-Carol Publishing, Inc.
PO Box 701
Johnson City, TN 37605
publisher@jancarolpublishing.com
www.jancarolpublishing.com

To my friends, whose days are enriched by their favorite friends, their pets.

And to Milo, my new roommate, who also happens to be a cat.

May all their lives be full of cuddles and wild playfulness!

Author's Note

Thank you for picking up my book.

Throughout my life, I've had my share of pets, including cats, dogs, and horses. I've also developed relationships with 4-H show calves, a few birds, fish in bowls, and even mice, the last of which unfortunately were killed by one of my cats before my science project was completed. I can't say I was ever the world's most patient and loving pet owner, but each made my life better than if I had only been around humans.

Now, in my elder years, I'm an onlooker as people and their pets prance by me, as I sit on a bench in downtown Asheville. This city seems like the place to go if you want to show off your dog (and once in a while, a cat). Daily we became a parade route for owners of perfectly groomed poodles, Cocker Spaniels, Yorkies, collies, nervous little chihuahuas in their knitted sweaters, Pomeranians settled into their pet strollers, and many other four-legged best friends of humans

Once in a while, I wonder if any of these perfectly behaved dogs have ever yearned to be rid of the collars and leashes, to be free to join the wide and wonderful playground of the wild, like a new generation of Jack London's dog hero, Buck, in *The Call of the Wild*, published in 1903.

This book's hero is Blackeye, because of the black spot surrounding one of her eyes. From her beginning as a newborn pup in a barn, she knows that domestic life is not for her, and the idea of being *fixed* is completely out of the question.

So, join Blackeye as she romps through the highs and lows of Appalachia, falls in love, and struggles to remain wild in a world that wants to tame and train her. And will it be worth eating cute little animals instead of gourmet food served in a pretty bowl with her name on it?

Foreword

During my recent years living in downtown Asheville, I've noticed that pet dogs are the new family members for both singles and couples who wander the wide sidewalks near my home. Many of the local merchants even provide fresh water in doggie bowls outside their stores. Others up the ante by offering doggie treats. In today's world, some dogs wear beautiful, freshly knitted sweaters. Some wear little slippers and are pushed in strollers.

I wanted to know how the individual dogs felt about their near humanization. Of course, none would tell me. Some would growl if I even asked. So, I made up my own dog, Blackeye. She likes being born into a litter of wild dogs. She rebels against what humans expect of her. One human even envies her independence. Blackeye dreams of the day when she can escape. But she doesn't think about finding her own food, being cold at night, or getting wet and blown about during storms. Would any dog? Or do dogs think, see, or hear like we do? Do they even see the same colors we do? What if a dog escapes into the wild before they're neutered? Do females have no say about with whom they will mate?

Can they ever be domesticated again? Blackeye will tell you. But remember, most dogs can't talk like my Blackeye.

Introduction

My name is Blackeye. I am a proud female dog, or as most people might call me, a bitch.

Before I relate my story to you humans and other creatures, let me tell you that I have also picked up a few human skills here and there since my humble birth. In this book, I can now describe to you how much I've been through in my short life so far. Let me tell you right now that I'm still more crazy about the wild than I am about wide sidewalks. And speaking of sidewalks, when will humans start doing better on the leash? I'm yet to see one who can keep up with me when I take them out for their walks.

My story includes few regrets. Yes, I'm unlike most dogs who have stayed with their owners. That wasn't for me. I needed my own life. I was determined to not be owned by anyone. Here's my story.

Chapter 1

I was born in a barn, one among six in the litter. My mother seemed to have never had a real home. My daddy dog skipped the county and left her to deal with her pregnancy by herself. I'm glad she found a barn in which to birth us, because it protected us from other hungry creatures out there who were searching for a meal in the middle of a January cold spell.

My mother may have, at first, believed that I didn't really belong in her litter with my brothers since I was the only female. They were all pitch black. I'm white with this funny little black spot around my right eye. No trouble picking me out in a crowd, that's for sure.

I don't remember much of my early days. But whenever I get into a barn and smell the manure, baled hay, and straw, I get this cozy feeling that I've been there before. I can almost taste the warm milk that I suckled from my mother as she gathered us around her engorged tits. Being the smallest of the litter, I vaguely remember being pushed away from one nipple and having to root around for another because my brothers were bigger and tougher than I. No big deal. I thrived during this short period of my life, and by the time we were discovered by the first human I ever saw, I was up to about the average individual weight of my brothers.

Not sure what that human thought of us when we were found. I'm sure that my life changed immensely beginning on that February morning when I heard a yell like a screech owl.

"Harry, c'mere!"

Nobody came. So, she yelled again. And again. Finally, I heard the squeaky door open and close, and footsteps thumping on the barn floor, spreading fine dust from the hay and straw and the little pellets of mouse and pigeon poop. A gravelly voice started with a gurgle in the human's throat, "What you want, woman? Whatchu doin' out here anyways? Shouldn't you be up in the house cookin' up some biscuits and gravy, 'stead of rummaging around out here in this ol' barn?"

"Just had a hankerin' to come out here and see if any of our hens decided to lay here since we ain't gettin' much eggs from the coop come lately."

"Well, find any?" the old human asked. "You know hens don't lay much in win'er."

"Nope, but come over here closer, and see what I done found 'tween these bales. I see some money comin' our way in a few weeks."

The old man drew closer and peered down at us pups. "Well, I'll be. Cute little fellers, ain't theys?"

The old woman grabbed me by my loose skin and looked at my butt. "Aw, a female! Think we can get much for her and the others?"

The old man nodded and slapped the old woman's behind. "Leave 'em alone, Glory. Their eyes ain't even quite open yet. Need some fillin' out a bit. For now, git back in the house and make some vittles. The little mama here will take care of the younguns."

The next couple of suns and moons passed by too soon. The old woman came back regularly and examined each of us, our butts, our paws. She opened our mouths and put her dirty finger down our throats. She lifted us up and dropped us to see if we would land on all fours. I didn't like this human. What right did she have to be in charge of our butts, mouths, paws, or tiny eyes?

You may say, "Well, that was just an uneducated woman who had no gentleness or respect for other species."

Maybe back then I would have given you the benefit of the doubt, since humans seem to be so smart. But today, I say that she was maybe a little kinder than others of the human species I've seen in my years of running away from people.

Chapter 2

Mama was a good nurturer. While I nursed from her every chance I got, she would clean my butt and comb my glistening coat with her rough tongue.

I loved her so much. I wanted to be just like her. I dreamed of staying with my mama the rest of my life. She would teach me how to hunt and how to evade the humans. Maybe someday I would have baby puppies myself, and my mama would teach me how to feed my babies. Meanwhile, I frolicked and wrestled with my brothers. I grew stronger and could feel my muscles begin to replace the fat on my four legs. Our world was the main floor of the barn. We would fall asleep in the sunlight that carved an angle through the east and west dirty windows of the barn. Life was good in our tiny straw world. But like all good things, the euphoria wouldn't last.

One morning, the old woman interrupted our wrestling match by chasing us around the barn, into the old stalls where cows used to be milked, through the little fenced-in areas for recovering cows after calving, between stacked-up bales of hay, and under the loose boards of the barn floor. Every time she got hold of one of us, she would stuff us into a plastic bag. She had three of them. Two of us per bag. Finally, I was the last one caught. Into the bag I went. She tied the top of each bag and toted us into her house that smelled of mold and coffee. At the time, I didn't know what caused the smell, only that it was awful.

Inside, she opened each bag and put us all together in a huge cardboard box that we couldn't begin to reach the top of even if we jumped. Five of our voices became a yelping country ballad, crying for Mama. And Mama wouldn't come. Was she out hunting? Had she been killed? Was she tired of us?

While I spent my time running in circles looking for holes to squeeze through, one of my brothers just lay still on the crumpled old newspaper. I nudged him. He didn't move. I licked his ears, which usually riled him. But this time, he didn't even wiggle. I figured he was tired from running from the old woman before she caught him. I left him alone and played with the other four. Yet even into the dark hours, my brother Rolf, as Mama called him, didn't budge. The other pups and I surrounded him, poking him with our wet, cold noses. We flipped him over on his side, and he stayed like that. The old woman, flashlight shining from her hand, also nudged and poked him.

"Harry, one's dead!" she yelled from the kitchen to the bedroom.

"Throw him out, Glory. Make a good meal for somethin' out there."

She took him away from us. I heard the screen door open, a thud, and then the door closed. I didn't know what death was then. That old so-and-so couldn't throw out my brother into the cold night! Would Mama come to rescue Rolf? Maybe that old woman would also throw us out, and Mama could carry us back to the barn and everything would be back to normal. I waited to be next. But the old woman just put a bowl of water in the box and went to bed.

All of us yelped and squealed and moaned and cried that night. No Mama to suckle from. No one to caress our unruly coats. We each began to smell of pee and poop. Eventually we learned that we could all form one big ball to keep ourselves warm the rest of the night. I was the last to yawn and yelp. Then, even I was asleep. But it wasn't restful. It was traumatic. I wanted my mama in the worst way. Why wouldn't she answer our calls? Where was she?

The old lady's face was the first thing I saw the next morning. She had a smile on her face. Maybe she was happy that we were all still alive. I wasn't happy.

She took the bowl of water out of the box and replaced it with a bowl of white liquid. It was supposed to be milk but tasted nothing like the milk from our mama's nipples. Just to moisten my mouth and soothe my throat after yelping all night, I forced myself to lick up a few drops of the liquid like my brothers showed me. Afterwards, I withdrew into a corner, closed my eyes, and waited for the old woman to carry in our mama. But she never did. She didn't seem to like us anymore. Not that she ever really did. She was getting us ready for something. I don't know what. We didn't belong to her. I could tell she didn't love us. But what did I know? I was just a puppy.

When the guy called Harry came back after his morning chores, he and the old woman drank their black liquid and ate their morning toast. Old Harry was still hungry and complained to the old woman. She in turn reminded him that since she had found us, they would be making some money off of us when she took us to town. Some kind of spring holiday was coming, and maybe the Easter bunny would bring us in baskets to little humans.

All of that woman's words made no sense to me. Money? Bunny? I knew nothing of these words. But they were used over and over, so I took them seriously. Whatever they meant, I realized that the old barn wasn't on the agenda. No mention of Mama. And Rolf? Would he ever come back?

We puppies again huddled in the corner of the smelly old box. The old lady put in another layer of crumpled up newspaper. We still couldn't reach the top of the box. We were prisoners of the humans. We were scared to death. Our short lives seemed to have been in vain. We would become feed for the chickens, the rats, the coons, and foxes. But why had the old woman brought us into her house? Money? Holiday? Baskets?

The days and nights went by with very little change in our lives. We started to wrestle a little just to pass the time. We were famished, so we ate whatever little bit of food she gave us. Within a few days, I was able to reach the top of the box. She hit my paw and said, "No."

I didn't like that word. And I didn't like the meanness in her voice when she said it.

On the final day, she grabbed each of us and put us in the kitchen sink where she washed us one by one. The water was winter cold. The soap she used stung our eyes. We shivered as she wrapped us in scratchy towels that smelled like her and Harry. She dumped us into an even bigger box, closed the top, and set the box in the back of their old contraption on top of rings that went round and around. I heard them call it a pickup.

Off to town we went. It was a bumpy trip, but at last we were out of that old house. And maybe at last we would be able to get away from the old woman and her "Harry" man.

Chapter 3

We puppies ended up at a busy corner in Radison County. The whole area smelled the same as the back of the pickup. Our tiny coughs and watering eyes drew *aw's* from the shoppers in downtown Carson.

Meanwhile, the old woman dug in her jacket pocket, looked around herself, and took a swig out of an old dirt-covered container. I think getting us out of the pickup bed tired her out, and the liquid called moonshine brightened her spirits, making her act goofy to all the passersby who couldn't wait to smother us with tight holds and slobbering kisses.

You see, at the time, I didn't know that humans came in all different sizes, ages, and personalities. I decided then and there that I didn't like any of 'em. *Give me my mama*, I thought, *and I'll be happy*. I didn't want to play with these two-legged critters, cuddle up with them, chase their little strings, or even look into their light or dark eyes.

I didn't know that I was up for sale on that corner under the little tree with leaves the size of mouse ears. Could these humans sell dogs? I didn't belong to anyone. Who could have the right to sell me so I could sleep with a strange little human who could kick me if she was in a bad mood, or cover my coat with sticky kisses if she was lacking love from her parents?

I crawled into the corner of the huge box, made like I was about to die, and tried to blend in with the bowl of milk nearby. Nevertheless, being the cutest of the puppies and having that dark mark around my left eye endeared me to dozens of stinkers. And I really mean that. I decided that the old barn smells were like fresh air compared to the toddlers and teens who begged their mommies and daddies to take me home.

What, leave my brothers? They were a part of me, just as Mama and Rolf had been. Were these people wanting me to be the only dog? I had no idea of a life without my bros. Would they keep me in a dang box like a captive animal? Would they eat me someday?

I heard the old woman ramble off numbers as the onlookers asked her questions. "How much?"

"Forty," she'd say.

"Got their shots?"

"Nope, that's up to you'uns."

"Can you come down to $25?"

"Nope. My price is set. You don't know how much I've had to spend on these puppies since their mama died in my barn."

My head went dizzy. Mama, dead? Was this true, or was the old woman lying to make a sale? I wasn't born yesterday. Maybe a few months ago, but I knew the facts. We were stolen from our mama. She was alive somewhere out there, waiting for us to find her.

A fat little girl with frizzy hair blowing in her eyes and tickling her nose while it absorbed the snot running out of it picked me up and squeezed me tight onto her shoulder. "I want this one, Mother. Don't you think she'll make a good friend for me?"

A *friend?* I asked myself. Let her get real friends. I'm a dog, last time I looked. I don't want to be a friend to a stupid little girl who would use me like a tissue to wipe her nose or absorb her tears when she couldn't get another cookie. I had a pretty good idea of what kids were like just by watching this one little girl. She seemed spoiled, a smart-aleck, whiny, and obnoxious. I looked over at the other pups, asleep together in their normal, big ball of shiny hair. They couldn't care less what was happening here. We were about to be separated, maybe forever. Too bad I had to be the smartest and the prettiest of the whole litter.

"I'll take thirty and no less," the old woman asserted. "And that's only because your little girl wants it so bad."

"Female or male?" the mother inquired.

"Female. You'd have to get her fixed if you don't want every male in the county scratching on your doors in a couple months."

"Oh, shucks. I don't think—"

"Mother, this is the one I want. And I don't want it fixed. It's perfect just as it is. We'll take it, ma'am."

The girl's mother looked stunned as she pulled lots of paper stuff from her purse.

At that moment, I was grabbed by the skin of my neck by the little girl named Sara and shoved into a stiff, otherwise empty bag that had stick figures on it. I didn't even get a chance to exchange sniffs with my brothers before our separation.

I had no idea what to expect after this. But then, so far for the last few weeks, I'd never had any idea what was around the corner. All I knew to do was let my grief out. I yelped and whined in the dark space of the bag that swung from Sara's arm. She decided to skip to keep up with her mama at the store with lots of gadgets in it. It was there that they chose the thing they put around my neck and the long rope that would haunt me the rest of my life. No running away with those things on me.

For my ride to my new home, I got to travel on the floor of the front seat of a moving thing called a car that moved on skinny black rings they called wheels. The ride was much smoother, and it smelled like some crazy leaf or root, which I found out later was cinnamon. Sara was the name of the little girl who sang along with loud sounds coming out of nowhere in the car. The mama drove the car higher up a mountain, curve after curve. I threw up sour milk. I heard the mama say in a gruff voice, "Just what I needed! Throw up in my new shopping bag. You would insist on a puppy today. Girl, you're going to have to take care of it from now on. I've never liked dogs. Good thing your dad does, because I would rather spit at it than look at it."

"Aw, Mother, you know you'll love little Blackeye. I already do. I'm gonna comb her, take her on walks, potty train her, and have tea parties with her. I'll put a ribbon around her ears, and she'll be the prettiest dog in Radison County. You'll see."

"Well, first we gotta get her shots and have her fixed," her mama insisted. "And if she poops or pees on the floor, you'll clean it up. If she yelps all night, I won't come and calm her down. That'll be up to your dad or you."

I heard it all, not exactly knowing what *shots* and *fixed* meant. But I did know that the mama didn't like me, and I didn't like her either. And the little girl, Sara? Oh my God, she was worse. Ribbons around my ears? Tea? Walks? I had to get out of this. If there was one thing I did know at this young age, it was that I was a dog, not a toy like little Sara seemed to think I was.

Upon arriving at Sara's home, I was amazed at the difference between her home and the old woman's. This house smelled like flowers and floor polish. I wasn't put in a box, but on a cushion in the shape of an egg. It was soft and smelled like a dog. I was to find out later that the family's cocker spaniel had died weeks before I came. Skittles was his name. I wondered if Skittles had enjoyed being a plaything for Sara. Did he die an early death? Was he bored to death? And how was I going to get along without my brothers? Were they being bought and sold, too, at this very minute?

Sara, as promised, brushed me with a grooming comb after washing the vomit from my hair. I ended up smelling like some more flowers. Then, she set a bowl of canned puppy food before me. I had to admit, I drooled. Saliva was dripping from my mouth. I gobbled up the whole bowl of food in a couple breaths. Within an equal amount of time, I threw it all up. Instead of Sara cleaning it up, her mama did, cursing the whole time, insisting that I probably had worms living inside me.

"Monday, that little gal goes to the vet," she told Sara. "I'm not having a worm-infested dog in my nice clean house."

Like she predicted, I did cry all night long. And who came to console me but Sara's mama. I had told myself that I couldn't stand the woman, but as the night went on, I began to think of her as a mama—not anywhere like my own, and yet a mama, who does all the caring.

The next day, Sara invited her girlfriends, puppies themselves in human terms, to come and see how cute I was. As she had promised the other little girls, she had me entertain them at a tea party, going so far as to tilt my head back, opening my mouth and pouring weak tea down my throat. Each girl was allowed to comb my hair and tie a rainbow of colored ribbons around the base of my ears. I took my little paws and tried my darndest to force the ribbons off my ears, but the efforts were futile.

When the girls became bored, they decided to put the new collar on me, and then to attach the leash to it. Time for a walk. I was tired. I wanted to crawl over to the cushion and take a nap. All puppies need their naps just like baby humans. But Sara and her friends would have none of that. She yanked me to my feet and dragged me out the door. The girls decided to race to the road at the end of the gravel driveway. My little paws were soft and fragile. I didn't have shoes on like the girls did. The gravel pieces hurt my feet, and I cried. The girls huddled around me, fighting over who would get to squeeze me the tightest.

Was this to be the story of the rest of my life? Was I going to be molded into some type of being that a human thought I should be? I told myself then that I would stay at this house, eat their food, and grow up. Then, I would run away and be who my mama wanted me to be.

The little girls finally had to go home. Each plastered a sticky kiss on my nose and ran to her mama's fancy wagon that took them away. By then, Sara was also ready for a nap herself. At last, I would get a little peace and quiet. I could mourn the loss of my mama and brothers, the old barn. I could savor the taste of the good dog food and whole milk I had here. The smell of pee and coffee was gone. I heard music coming from the kitchen that soothed me for some reason. And then I was gone into another world—a world of puppies biting and wrestling with me. Jumping over me. We were fighting over our mama's bulging tits, and I felt her gentle cleaning of my butt and the combing of my black spot with her tongue. All was well in our doggie family. If there was a Creator in the air somewhere, it was watching over us so we could grow up to one day be proud and beautiful dogs ourselves. We would walk in our mama's paw prints. We would discover all the wonders of the world, chase rabbits and squirrels, watch worms come out and go back into their earthen holes. And we would always be together, because we were a pack, and that was more important than anything else on this earth.

Chapter 4

The night after the tea party and the walk on the jagged gravel was a painful night for me, even though the house was quiet, smelled like the humans' dinner, and my cushion was soft. My poor paws tingled. I wasn't yet used to running to keep up with humans who had been here much longer than I had. My throat was raw from the tea that was poured into it. I wanted to sleep, but when I closed my eyes, my pain was unbearable, so I cried for my mama. Of course, she didn't come. But Sara's mama did. I could see that she was also tired and wanted me to shut up. Instead, I nestled my little head in the crook of her arm. I could feel her blood rushing back and forth to her heart, a little bit like what I felt when I fell asleep at Mama's breast.

Don't get me wrong. I still didn't like humans. Not a single one of them, not even Sara's mama. I knew she would have rathered I was not there in her house. It was too clean for a messy little girl like me. Nevertheless, we did share some feelings. We felt trapped in the immaculate showcase of a house looking down to the old river valley. Even she wanted to be free, and she was a human mother. I wondered how much she had given up to be the matriarch of this castle. I know I had given up too much, but it wasn't my choice. This was her choice, and she was regretting it, I bet.

Sara woke us both up just as the sun was spitting its rays of light between the trees and their little buds. She didn't think of announcing her presence with a sweet whisper or anything like that. No, she wanted to play. This morning, I would learn to fetch her rubber ball and bring it back to her so she could throw it again, and I would fetch it again over and over until I puked.

Breakfast first, however. Sara chose colorful little circles that floated around in a bowl of milk. I got half a can of the dog food I had yesterday. I assumed I got less so I wouldn't overeat and throw it all up again. I licked the bowl clean and washed it all down with a tiny bowl of warm milk.

Sara's daddy then made his appearance. His hair was sticking up in every direction. Sara left me and went to sit on her daddy's lap. She played with his pajama buttons and planted kisses on his face and hands. I thought about that for a while. Was that what daddies were for? I wondered what happened to my daddy. Could I be the one who looked like him?

"Isn't she about the cutest puppy you've ever seen, Daddy?" Sara asked. "Do you like her name, Blackeye? I'm teaching her to catch a ball and bring it back. Do you think I should teach her to sit and shake hands? Maybe roll over? I want her to grow up to protect us from robbers and mean people. But I want her to be nice to us too. Will you help me teach all those things?"

"Sara, baby, you know I'm busy with my job right now. Let's just let her grow up a little more, huh? We have lots of time. Mother said you wore your puppy out yesterday. You gotta be gentle with 'em. Will you promise me that you'll be gentle?"

"Ah, Daddy, she likes it. She likes to play with me. Watch her chase the ball."

She threw the yellow ball over to the fireplace. I stayed put, pretending that I didn't see anything. No way was I going to cater to that little spoiled brat. She pouted and threw it again. And I stayed put.

"I guess I'll have to work harder on this," she announced as she went back to her dad's buttons, one by one buttoning them up again.

The rest of the day seemed to go on and on forever. Sara was determined that I learn how to sit, shake hands, run around in circles, jump higher and higher until I reached her shoulder. She even wanted me to bark like her.

"No, not a yelp, a bark like this," she would instruct. In turn, I would yelp and whine to let her know that I was the dog, and not she. I was beginning to plan my escape by dinnertime, but the dog food changed my mind.

That night, Sara begged her mother and daddy to let me sleep in her bed. I couldn't believe it. I could see how she would crush me during the night. I quietly left the conversation and hid in the food pantry close to the cans of dog food which I loved almost as much as my real mama.

During the time I was hiding, Sara lost the battle of having me sleep with her. Instead, she was allowed to stay up half an hour later so she could play with me. She brought out her little baby buggy, threw her doll out on the floor, and wrapped me up in a bright yellow blanket with blue satin around its edges. She dumped me in the empty baby buggy and squealed around the house, pushing me into as much furniture as she could, tipping it over half a dozen times and yelling at the top of her lungs that she loved me so-o-o much. If I had been able to talk, I would have told her to soak her head in the toilet.

Finally, finally, she ran out of steam and was tucked into her frilly bed with the unicorn spread on it. She said her prayers while her daddy listened. She chose me to be blessed first. The only blessing I wanted was an open door and a road that would take me back to Mama, wherever she was.

After Sara was thoroughly tucked in, kissed by both parents, assured that the monsters had all vacated her room, and after one more kiss on my ticklish nose, we all marched out of her room into civilization. But there would be one more lesson before I would be allowed to slumber as well.

Sara's mother had put down little white pads with blue trimming by the door leading to outside. I decided to play dumb as she explained that I was to go pee on one of those pads instead of other places, like under the kitchen table, alongside my cushion, by Daddy's recliner in the living room, or at the bottom of the stairs.

The mother was so serious, and I was so dumb, that the entire episode seemed wasted. I was a dog. I couldn't use that thing where they pooped and peed, so I would go wherever I darned wanted to. By Daddy's recliner was my favorite. It was their job to clean up after me for as long as I played dumb. They knew that since I was so beloved by Sara, they would have to tolerate my bad habits until I decided it was no fun anymore. So there.

While the mother continued her diatribe, I lumbered over to my cushion, encircled the inner edge a few times, and then curled up and went to sleep. Would I yelp and get Sara's mother up tonight? We'd see. No promises one way or the other.

Chapter 5

Darn, I slept through the night. All because of Sara wearing me out with the dangerous joy ride in the baby buggy. First thing the mother did was check the pads she put out the night before. They were all dry, but I really had to go. I wanted to go outside, but she wouldn't open the door for me. Accidentally, I peed on the pad and got sweet praises and what humans call a treat. My teeth were still coming in, so I mostly sucked on the little hard morsel until it dissolved in my mouth. Not worth the effort, I decided, so I spit it all out on the carpet, where the human obediently scrubbed it out.

"Today we're taking you to the vet," the mother warned me.

Hmm, the vet. So, what was a vet? Was I going to be sold to this vet? Was he a friend or a mean old human who wanted to eat me? Should I escape now? This place had good food, but that little girl of theirs was driving me mad. Maybe the vet would be a tiny bit better. I would take my chances.

Just then, out from her bedroom bounced Sara, once more full of kisses and bone-crushing hugs. She attached the leash to my itchy collar and made me sit by her chair while she ate her floating nuggets and drank the uckly liquid they floated in. Then, it was time to run around the house, slipping and sliding at each corner, being dragged from the kitchen to the dining room to the living room, up the stairs and down, getting a break as she sat on the big white bowl in the bathroom. Then, she flushed and scared me to death. Was the house going to fall into the ground? Was a monster down there where her pee went? Then, she dragged out a tiny stool, stood on it, and washed her little paws with long claws painted pink. I was glad to get out of that strange room, even if I had to be dragged through the house again.

The mother went upstairs and got into some other clothes. She looked at herself in a window that looked just like her face. She smiled at the face, and the face smiled back. She washed her face, and so did the person in the window. It copied everything she did. I wondered when she would slap it for being a copycat. Instead, she put some stuff the color of her skin all over her face, some dark marks around her eyes, and something like blood paste on a stick to her lips. Of course, the woman in the window copied her again.

I yelped at the person in the window to just leave. Was I becoming protective of this human? Naw. Just tired of watching the mother have no guts to kick that woman out of her bathroom.

We all got in the car. Sara and I sat in the back seat. She had to wear a seat belt, and her job was to hold me so I didn't jump around and bother her mother, who was driving the car.

Down the mountain, curve after curve we went. I looked outside, hoping I would see Mama come out of the woods along the way. I didn't see her, but I seemed to see everything else. Sara explained that the big, fat, black thing was a bear, and the being that ran across the road with tree limbs on his head was a deer. I saw dead beings, too. She called them a skunk, an opossum, and a raccoon. I realized then that if I ran away—when I did run away—I would avoid these killing roads. Tears ran down my face. And yes, we dogs do have tear ducts, mostly to clean our eyes. But sometimes I just cry.

Then, at last, the mother stopped the car in front of a small building. "We're here," she announced to Sara. "Your job is to keep Black-eye on your lap until the vet's nurse calls us into the examination room."

"Okay, Mother," Sara replied. I could see that this time around, they were a team, and I was the victim. I started to shake. As soon as the mother opened the door, I felt faint. A whiff of chemical smells invaded my nose. I coughed my little puppy cough. Big dogs barked at me. I wondered if any of them were my daddy.

But the most vicious were members of another species. They hissed at me, arched their backs, and lashed out with their paws like they wanted to scratch me. I was in a den of terror. What had I done to be brought here? Did vets punish animals who disobeyed and peed on floors? All the more reason to run away from this life with humans.

Chapter 6

My little heart shook my entire body as the three of us sat in the waiting room's slick, shiny chairs. I noticed images of other dogs and those other hissing animals all over the walls. Were these animals still alive or had this vet eaten them? I had no idea what was behind that door other than a young woman with a clipboard in her hands.

Within a few minutes, Sara poked me as the woman called out, "Blackeye." Of course, that was me. I wanted to disappear. Maybe I could be one of those animals on the wall or I could run away at this moment.

Instead, I froze like an ice cube in my water dish. I was being pulled into the vet's office, yelping all the way with my brakes on. Sara's mother set me on top of a shiny, slick, tall table, on which my legs spread out in all directions. Was this where humans slaughtered animals? Was this family mad at me because I didn't want to use those pads to pee on? Was it my time to be sacrificed to the vet gods?

I heard the mother, Mrs. Gregg, and the vet talk about weird-sounding conditions like rabies and heartworm. She nodded along with the vet. Then, the worst came. I saw a needle aimed straight at me.

"Ouch," I yelped. Was I going to die now? Sara took me in her arms. I didn't want Sara. I wanted my mommy.

"You're going to be okay, Blackeye. I get shots all the time. They say that there's medicine they put into you that protects you from bad sicknesses."

Sure, I thought. *That's what they probably all say.* Maybe we're really getting stuff that will make us sick. I thought I was going to throw up there on the table. But I just peed a little bit and slid on the yellow puddle beneath me.

Time to go home, I tried to communicate to Sara, but she was listening to her mother and the vet talk about *fixing* me. I perked up my ears to find out what that meant.

"She's too young right now to be spayed," the vet explained to Sara's mother.

Spayed? What in tarnation was that? Wasn't *fixing* me enough? I didn't need either, I was convinced. I had to run away the next time that kitchen door opened.

"Later we'll make an appointment for your little lady to get back before she comes into heat. Then, I'll do the surgery," the vet man reassured Sara's mother.

I was listening to all of this. Once more, words were being thrown around that I had no knowledge of. However, Mrs. Gregg and the vet guy were so serious. Mrs. Gregg took out a pretty stick and put the sharpest tip of it in a tiny book-like thing. The stick left a track like water running down a hill, a turn and loop here and there, but this track was across instead of up and down.

I could feel that this conversation would someday have a big impact on my life. I shuddered.

Sara's mother put her hand on my head, much more gently than her daughter ever did. I had to remind myself that I didn't like her or any other humans, all of whom thought nothing of separating me from my mama and brothers. And this *surgery* thing, this *fixing*, this *spaying*, when I got *heated*. I was sure pain was coming my way as soon as I got hot. And were these actions going to make me less of a dog? I think the word that scared me most was *fixing*. Thanks, but no thanks. I was fine just as my mama made me, and my daddy, too, wherever either of them were today. Maybe they were making a new family to replace us.

The vet looked at my butt. But he didn't smell or lick it like we dogs do to each other. I've even tried to smell Sara, thinking her smell would tell me why she's so mean most of the time.

After my butt, the vet forced my mouth open. I gagged and coughed. Then, he took a cold, gray, round thing hanging from his neck and put it on my chest. He looked at my paws and said, "Looks like the puppy's paws have been scratched almost raw."

Mrs. Gregg looked down at Sara, and Sara looked at the wall that had nothing on it. This time, I nodded.

"I'll give you some salve to put on the paws so that they don't get infected," the vet said. "Little girl, remember that little puppy was born just a few months ago. She's still a baby. Handle with care."

"A deal, Doctor." Her small hand clasped his big, hairy one.

That was quite a trip for me, so I fell asleep on Sara's lap on the way home. The purr of the car's motor reminded me of the heartbeats of Mama and my brothers. When I closed my eyes, there we were in that old barn. I was warm and cozy again. Mrs. Gregg turned down the volume on that thing that had noise coming out of it, and my world was perfect one more time.

Chapter 7

All the perfection of the warm nap with pleasant dreams ended dramatically with a bump, bang, crash, boom, screech, rattle, and roll. Then, there was nothing. Not even screaming. My dreams went from a sweet dream to a horrible nightmare in slow motion.

The next thing I heard was a screeching, loud, horn-like noise coming from a vehicle with an enclosed little hut on the back of it. It stopped with a squealing noise while a light on top of it kept blinking. All three of us were in different stages of waking up from the wreck. We'd hit a bigger pickup than the one the old woman who gave me away drove. It must have taken up most of the road on one of its many curves.

One female and two male humans looked at Mrs. Gregg's big car, which seemed to hang from the edge of the mountain. One of the males said they needed back-up and a rope. Meanwhile, I think all three of us were on the pathway to death. I started my puppy yelp and whine. I'd never been so spooked.

The female helper started to cry when she saw me. "Aww, you hear that puppy in the backseat? We gotta go in and save it right now!" she yelled. "If a puppy dies in this crash, we'll be driven out of town. Let's get in there pronto."

The two men perked up when they witnessed her unusual compassion. Me and Sara, being so small and still in Sara's seatbelt, were released from the vehicle with no problems. But getting Mrs. Gregg out was quite an ordeal. She wasn't screaming, talking, whining — not anything. *Maybe she was dead like my brother*, I thought. But even I, a dumb little puppy, knew better than to put that thought in Sara's mind.

Another vehicle with a light on top of it came and took us to a place where they put hurt people. Seems they called it an *emerging* van. When they saw that I wasn't a person, they started to take me out of the van, but Sara refused to stay in it without me. I really wanted the helping people to pick her up kicking and screaming and put her in another van. I could have gotten a break from her mean ways. But they thought we were in love, I guess.

A woman, dressed like the vet who saw me earlier, examined Sara. She didn't smell her butt, though, which would have told her much more. For one thing, Sara had peed and pooped on me because of the accident. I kept all my stuff inside me because we dogs are stronger and braver than humans. That's why we live in barns and caves. I needed a bath. I couldn't stand the idea that a human, even a little girl, had messed me with her icky stuff. She'd even thrown up on me.

Sara wouldn't release me. As a matter of fact, she started squeezing me tighter and tighter till I could hardly breathe. The woman looking her over finally saw how I couldn't breathe.

"Everything's going to be okay for you and your pet, Sara," she stressed. "Now, your puppy needs to breathe. Loosen up a bit, please."

She let go of me. I didn't move right away. I had to catch my breath first. Then, I was out of there, running down the hall as fast as my little furry legs would carry me. Then, right in front of me was a closed double door. I looked from side to side. No way to escape. I decided to hide under a chair in the waiting room, planning to make a quick dash as soon as someone came through the doors.

No one came. My eyes started getting heavy and heavier. Before I knew it, I was gone again into dreamland where life was simpler and quieter, where horrible smells didn't exist and where I could just lie around and grow between sucking warm plentiful Mama's milk and a good wrestle with bros.

I was in the middle of a battle with the biggest of them, and I was waving one paw in celebration, when I was grabbed by a big, rough hand. "About time we found you," Sara's father said with relief. "We're going home now."

Oh no, I thought. Sara was at Mr. Gregg's side.

"When will Mother come home?" Sara asked her father. Mr. Gregg just kept walking. Sara asked again and turned to go toward the emergency room, but her father started dragging her, much like Sara would drag me.

Strange, I thought. Why is Mrs. Gregg not with us? What happened to her? Oh well, none of my business. I'm out of this town in a few weeks anyway, before I go to that vet and get fixed.

We rode in Mr. Gregg's pickup, a modern version of the old one the old woman used to take me to town before I was sold. That thought again made me wonder, isn't there something wrong with selling other living creatures? Seems I heard about that on the news one night. I think the announcer called it trafficking. But, of course, he was talking about the humans, not dogs like me.

"We're going to let Mother stay in the hospital for a few days," Mr. Gregg explained to Sara after we got on the road. "Mother was hurt from the accident worse than you and Blackeye. We'll pray that she gets better real soon, starting tonight."

"Are you sure Mother's getting better?" Sara asked. "Her face had lots of blood on it, and she acted like she was asleep when the lifesavers took us to the hospital. They will make her better, won't they, Daddy?"

"I'm sure they'll do their best, honey," was all he said.

Sara's grandmother came later that day. She didn't look or act or speak like Sara's mother. She had smoke coming out of her nose and mouth from before the sun came up to the time when the moon showed its glow. She didn't like me, and to tell the truth, I hated her more than

Sara. She yelled at both of us whenever we crossed her path. Both Sara and I were happy when Mr. Gregg came home. He ruled the house. All of a sudden, Mrs. Gregg's mother would become quiet, doing her cooking and eating and washing dishes. Then, Mr. Gregg would put Sara to bed, and Sara's grandma would talk real serious to Mr. Gregg about her daughter.

"Doesn't look good," he would say.

"Well, things gotta improve. I can't spend the rest of my life taking care of Sara. I'm a sick woman and need to be home. Jennifer just needs to do her physical therapy like those doctors will tell her to do, and in no time at all, she'll be back to normal."

"It's not that simple," Mr. Gregg replied. "She has serious brain and spinal injuries. Two strikes against her to get those legs independent. Oh, she wants to walk like everyone else, but certain parts of her body won't communicate with one another."

"That's all a bunch of hogwash," Mrs. Gregg's mother insisted. "I'm going over to that hospital tomorrow and telling her to get with the program. She's got a little girl out here who needs her mommy."

"Don't you dare talk to my wife like that. She's trying." Mr. Gregg gave her a mean look. "If you don't want to help us out, help your daughter out. If you can't at least do that, then you can leave tomorrow. We'll get along fine without you. I'll work from home and get this place ready for a wheelchair. Pack your bags tonight, and we'll bid you goodbye tomorrow."

That old smoking woman, she looked real gruff. She got out of that chair, turned sharply around, and marched into the spare bedroom.

I looked at Mr. Gregg and went to my little cushion. I wasn't going to do anything to get that man mad at me, too. He was too big for me to deal with.

Chapter 8

Mr. Gregg did just fine when Mrs. Gregg's mother moved out. He made all of Sara's meals from boxes and see-through bags. She didn't complain much because he didn't make her eat any of that stuff that grew from plants like her mother had done.

One night as Sara was finishing dinner and getting ready to bother me for a few hours, her father told her to stay put for a few minutes. "We're going to get Mother tomorrow. She will get around here in a wheelchair and a walker. You need to keep your toys picked up and not bother your mother too much. Don't ask her about the scars on her face. We'll get them fixed. She'll also have some trouble reaching for things, so you have to help. Can you do that, honey?"

"Sure," Sara answered. "Whoopie, Blackeye, Mother's coming home tomorrow! Ain't that awesome?"

All I did was bark like the good little dog she thought I was. I would be a tiny bit happy to see Mrs. Gregg back. She was the most like me of anyone in the family. I could tell by her eyes that she wanted to be free of this life and be free like the wild animals such as the black bears we saw scampering along the road with their cubs.

But this time she would be in a wheelchair. I guessed that meant she'd have wheels below her butt instead of legs. Would she be happy, sad, or mad?

The next day I found out. She was sad—extremely sad. She would look at me often during the day like I was supposed to save her. She knew I didn't like living as a pet. I didn't want to get fixed. I just wanted to be a real dog with no leashes, no collars, a bed out in a barn or in a cave, anywhere but in this fancy house that didn't smell wild.

Of course, we couldn't really talk. I could see that Mrs. Gregg still had her legs. But they didn't work very well. The wheels on the wheelchair took her here and there. On her better days, she was on her walker. Within a few days of coming home, she'd fallen five times. She wasn't a wild animal like me. She needed her house, her husband, her child. Did she also think she needed me?

Well, maybe I could cheer her up during the time Sara was in school. I jumped up on her lap while she watched the talking, moving screen. I let her pet me and scratch my neck. All the while, I was planning my escape. But I didn't want to leave her a total mess. Even dogs want people to be happy.

I realized, even while still a pup, that I was confused about my role in all of this upheaval going on in the Gregg family. Was it my job to make the mother happy? When I couldn't stand her sadness, I would sometimes jump off her lap and go over to the window—the one I could reach by getting on my hind legs—and look out at the chirping and fluttering birds. Were they flying around to entertain the rest of us? How would they feel if they were caught and had to live in a cage? Would they still sing? No, they'd probably cry. They wouldn't be free.

Summer was coming. I was getting much bigger. Why, I could probably take care of myself soon.

One day, I heard Mrs. Gregg on her phone. I couldn't believe my ears. She was asking someone somewhere if it was about time to get Blackeye (*me!*) fixed.

No way! I stomped (as much as a little dog can stomp) to within inches of her chair. I looked in her eyes and shook my head left and right. I whined and yelped. She thought I needed to go outside to pee. She wheeled over to the kitchen door and opened the screen door. I was free to leave to pee or poop. But as I walked beyond the threshold,

I looked forward and backward. Was this the time to leave? I could. She couldn't chase me. Mr. Gregg was at work and Sara was at school. I was free to go. Maybe she knew that. Maybe she also knew I wanted to leave for good, and she was going to help me. Maybe she didn't like me after all. Or maybe she was showing me that she did indeed love me.

Hey, this was ridiculous. Now I was even beginning to think like humans. No real dogs think like humans. Wild dogs and some domesticated dogs think like dogs. They make humans happy so they'll get food and drink. They become dependent on humans.

But love them? Naw. I don't love these people in this house. I use them and I'm tired of being dependent on them. I'm leaving right now.

I ran beyond the fenced-in yard. I was fascinated by the woods before me. I smelled cool water running from the spring out in those woods. I was free at last. No fixing would happen to me. It was time to move on.

Before I knew it, there I was by the biggest tree in the backyard near the woods behind it. The old oak tree was about to fully leaf out. She was dancing to the breeze, ruffling her emerging leaves. She stood far above all the trees near her. The others seemed to be bowing, and she waved her most flexible branches at them as though she were inspiring them to show their stuff.

Gazing up at the trees, I felt happy. I'd done it. I'd moved out. Where would I sleep tonight? No outbuildings around. These were just city people who liked wide open spaces away from other people. A little bit like me, come to think of it.

I knew I had to find some place to sleep tonight. So, I started to do some "home" hunting. I drank from the spring. Would sure like to have a domicile close to the spring. In case I got thirsty, I could walk outside and take a few sips of cold mountain water. I used my nose to follow some scents. I searched under last year's leaves on the ground. But I couldn't find anything suitable. Hmm. Where was there a second option? Over under the inspiring oak? Maybe I would like listening to her leaves whistle in the wind, or snuggling up to her trunk, feeling it expand while I slept. I could push lots of leaves on one side of her, and then I would burrow into the leaves and sleep all night long.

I made my way back to the old oak and started using my nose to push leaves toward the tree. This was the hardest I'd worked in my life. Then, I jumped about three feet in the air as I heard steps coming closer to me. I could run, but I'd forgotten how. I became like a possum staring into car lights. I froze. Then, I discovered that I was being scooped up and scolded by Sara, who had come looking for me after she got home from school.

My senses came back, and I struggled to get out of her arms. But just as I had grown in recent months, so had Sara. She won. She dropped me when we got inside the kitchen door. And that was the end of my first little adventure as a free dog. I was disappointed, but I'd learned a lot in those few minutes. When I would leave, I'd need something to sleep in that was safe and hidden. I needed a water source, and I needed to think quickly on my feet. Put the possum behind me.

Chapter 9

So, I slept on my sweet cushion in a safe house where no one would intentionally hurt me. But just because no one intends to hurt you doesn't mean you don't get hurt. A hurt that was meant for good could hurt just as badly or worse than a hurt imposed on me because someone wished me harm. I'm thinking of Sara dangling me from a leash from the deck of the house, or a vet's knife piercing my insides so I'd be fixed.

I pushed my fears aside for another night so I could sleep soundly before another rough day ahead. Then, sometime after the darkest hour, when even the nocturnal animals were calling it a night, I heard some noises in the bathroom. Were there mice in this house? Never noticed them before. Z-z-z-z. Another noise in the bathroom. Bottles crashing into the sink. Someone, a woman, saying, "Shit."

I realized that if I was everything a dog was said to be, then I had to get up and put my protective face on. I pranced into the bathroom ready to use my canine teeth against a home invader. I saw a shadow creeping out of the bathroom. It was the shadow of a wheelchair with a woman in it. The woman had found what she was looking for and was gobbling down a handful of what I thought were treats with a glass of water.

Looking back, I thought this was strange, but I didn't think any great harm would come from what Mrs. Gregg was doing. Humans seemed to always be opening little bottles and swallowing little treats with some water before bed or after meals. I guessed she'd forgotten to take her treats before bed that night. I looked up at her, and our eyes locked. Sad eyes.

She made a sucking noise with her mouth and teeth, patting her lap for me to come sit. I preferred my cushion, but I knew what she wanted. So up on her lap I jumped. She gave me a smile like I'd never seen before. Her sad eyes were now sleepy eyes, as were mine. I assumed that her treats helped lessen her pain so she could sleep. I know I was ready to doze off again in the quiet of the night.

I felt her stroking my fur. If I closed my eyes, I could imagine my mama stroking my coat when I was about the size of a mouse. Her strokes soothed me like Mama's.

Then, she got gabby on me.

"Blackeye, you and me, we know each other, don't we? I have to admit Sara has no concept of how you feel, but I know you. You want to be free, don't you? I say, go for it. Don't get pushed into the middle of our human drama. I may have all the comforts of life—a great child, a kind husband. Then, why do I feel so damn awful? Is it this chair, my scars? My future? Maybe a little bit of all that. But basically, I'm imprisoned in this monstrosity of a house. It doesn't care about me, but I'm expected to care for it as though it's a part of me. I saw how you looked at those birds out there yesterday. I looked, too. You escaped. I only wanted to follow you. But this chair—

"Basically, little girl, I love you because you remind me of myself. And that's why I let you go. You didn't make it then, but you will someday. I'll be with you in spirit, guiding you. I'll be a wild woman at last. I don't want to change you, but I want to be with you for all your adventures as a free species. Will you let—"

Her voice teetered off to less than a whisper. Her hand stopped moving down my back. I fell asleep on her lap. A while later, when I could see that daylight was about to come, the lap I was on and her hand still on my back—they were both cold.

I didn't know what to do. This woman who had wanted me to be a wild species had me clamped between her heavy cold hand and her unmovable lap. It was then that I realized probably Mrs. Gregg was gone. She had entered the spirit world at last, as free as the birds that were now beginning to sing.

I started to yelp as loud as I'd ever yelped. Soon little Sara was up. She stood about a chair's length from us. Then, she was yelling for her daddy.

He came. He didn't yell. He searched for a pulse on his wife's neck and wrist. He lifted an eyelid and gazed into her eye. He didn't say or utter a word. He ran to his phone and called, I guess, those humans who drive vans with blinking lights on top.

Meanwhile, Sara pushed me off her mother's lap, climbed where I had sat, and sat in my spot. She stretched her arms out to encircle her mother's waist. Her mother's body slumped to the side of the wheelchair. Sara caressed her mother's arm, put her fingers in her mother's hair, and traced with her finger around the outer edge of her mother's lips.

"Mother, talk to me. Wake up, Mother."

We heard silence only. She rubbed the soft, cold skin that enclosed her mother. She tried to pinch her flesh. No response from her mother. One more time, she put her arms around her mother's waist and moved her hug up to her mother's shoulders. Tears were coming from Sara's eyes. She began softly to utter, "Mother," and then, in a crescendo, she said, "Mother," louder and louder until she was screaming as loud as a little girl could scream, "MOTHER!"

Then, her father was beside her. He pried her away from her dead mother, unlocking the crying little girl's fingers from around her mother's neck.

"Daddy, she's just asleep. Wake her up. You can do that. Kiss her real hard like I've seen you do before. C'mon, kiss her. She's just asleep. Isn't she? Isn't she? She'll wake up. It's still early. She was so tired last night. Take her to bed and cover her up nice and warm. She'll wake up."

"Baby, some people are coming to get Mother. If anyone can help her, they can."

Her daddy looked so sad, but I guess he didn't want Sara to see him cry. It seemed like forever before the people came to see Sara's mother. They did much the same things that Mr. Gregg had done. They didn't say, "Don't worry, sir. She'll be okay once we get her to the *hurt people* place. Just follow us and we'll have her up and about with no problem."

No, it was a grim situation. They, too, looked sad like Mr. Gregg. They shook their heads like they wanted to say, "Sorry, we can't do anything. She's deader than a doornail."

The three big people gathered into a circle and said lots of quiet, long words. Sara returned to her mother's side and started to play with the ring on Mrs. Gregg's finger. One more time, she used her fat little fingers to comb her mother's hair, stepped back, and approvingly smiled at her.

"I don't care what those people over there are saying. They don't know nothin'. I know you're just asleep, or maybe I'm having a bad dream. You'll be okay. You just need a rest. It's hard to not have legs that work very good anymore." Now, the tears were streaming from her eyes. "I promise I'll help you with your exercises. Soon, we'll be walking again, and we'll throw this old chair in the junk pile."

She kicked the wheelchair, and her mother's body slumped down in it even more.

"These nice people here, Sara, are going to take Mother now. We can see her later," Mr. Gregg said with tears in his eyes. "Now, move back a little, so they can put her on this stretcher. Sara. Sara! Move over."

"Daddy, they can't take Mother away while she's sleeping. Tell them to come back later when she's awake."

"Sara, Mother is dead. Do you understand? I don't understand myself, but she has died, and we'll see her later at the funeral home.

You'll have more chances to say goodbye to her in the next couple days. But there's not anything we can do for her now. Now, move over and let the nice people do their job."

I don't think he really wanted to yell at his little girl.

That's when I started my yelping and whining. Sara came over and clung to me. She was now petting me, saying nice words to me. And all the while, I was hearing the words of her mother that she had uttered before she died. I had to be of the wild species. But how could I leave this little girl now? Even a dog wouldn't do such a thing.

Chapter 10

This wasn't anywhere like the emergency a few weeks ago when Mrs. Gregg had been seriously injured in the car crash. This was Death, big DEATH, from which there is no cure, reprieve or hope. I missed Mrs. Gregg, but I wondered why she'd chosen to spend her last hours with me instead of her human family. Probably she'd known she could tell me anything and I wouldn't argue with her. And that was probably because I hadn't hardly understood what she was talking about anyway. Nevertheless, I was glad I had been a sounding board for her in her last hours.

One thing I did catch from her long speech was her encouragement to follow my desire to join the wild animals. I knew that was where I belonged.

But what to do now? Even my puppy conscience wouldn't allow me to desert Mrs. Gregg's family during this deep time of need. How long would it take for things to get back to a new normal in this bereaved family with no mama? The daddy in this situation performed like a machine, as long as nobody talked to him. The little girl, meanwhile, was used to a nurturing mother. Her daddy was rough around the edges in this situation. Blackeye—in other words, me—had to bring these two opposite poles into some sort of combination that would gel.

So, I was ready to give it some time. But there was a limit to how far I was willing to go. For now, I would submit to being dragged around the house and yard, being dressed up like a doll, and sitting through endless tea parties.

After the funeral, after the many gazes Sara gave to her mother in the pretty, shiny, wooden box, when she started staying at home long-term, she hung on me. She'd retire to her mother's bed, which still smelled like Mrs. Gregg. She'd throw her arm over me and explain what was going on, how her mother had died and gone to heaven and how someday she'd go to heaven, too, and stay with Mother forever. So, in the meantime, she had to work on being good. And it would be much easier for her to be good if I was good, too.

"No more peeing or pooping on the floor, Blackeye." She shook her index finger at me. "We need to keep you clean. The yelping at night must stop. You'll sleep with me. I'll teach you how to sleep soundly. And we need to not bother Daddy. He's got a lot on his mind, so let's not get in his way." Then, she'd smile and make a promise. "If you do all that, I'll have Daddy take you to the doggie spa as a reward."

Oh, please, I growled to myself, *spare me from ever going to one of those fancy places the humans think are so cool.*

But I would shake my head as though I understood her, while at the same time planning my big getaway. Each day I got closer to that goal. I would wake up, look at the birds flying from tree to tree, and let my heart fly with them—with the wind, against the wind, accelerating and gliding. I was ready. Someday this little girl at my side would have to be ready, too.

As I thought about my getaway, I began to draw a timeline in my mind. No matter what condition Sara was in at the time, once they took me to the vet again, I would make my fast dash to freedom in order to avoid being fixed.

For too many moons after Mrs. Gregg's death, we stayed in a howling and crying stage. I remembered that she had talked to the vet's office the day before she died. So, I knew an appointment had been set. And I was ready, but not in the way the humans thought.

Sara had to go to school sometime, and Mr. Gregg had to devote some time to his real job as a salesman. So, when both were out of my hair, I would have to sneak outside when the door hadn't closed completely, or when someone reached out to get those things in a box outside. I would then run like one of those animals with tree limbs on their heads. I learned to jump high, to dash farther and faster, to crawl under low objects. I was fit as a fox.

Then, it happened. I got moody. I snapped at Sara, even though I tried to be nice so she could recover from her mother's death. I found that I was licking my rear end more than usual. Maybe I did need to get *fixed* after all. Was I starting to fall apart? Was I going to die, too? Why me?

Oh, how I wished I had another dog to talk to. I didn't want to go to that vet, because he wanted to cut me somewhere. No one ever really said that, but I'd seen some of his silver instruments. No vets for me—ever!

The next day, while Sara was at school and Mr. Gregg was out selling whatever brought in the money, for some reason, the front door wasn't closed completely, so I went on a walk to places my nose led me. I was on a search for fellow dogs. It didn't matter, male or female. All that was important was that they be smart and older than me and have lots of dog sense.

I knew there were dogs in the neighborhood somewhere. I had heard them barking early in the mornings and at twilight. I hadn't seen any hanging around our place, so it was up to me to hang out at their places.

I had always walked like I was a proud canine. By now, I was about as big as the mama bear I'd seen on my trip to the vet. But I was lean and sleek. My ears stood straight up and at attention. Even though, today, my strut was a little off and my behind tickled, I was a pretty female. That's what Sara said anyway. My tail, which usually curled up like a spiral over my butt, was off to one side, however. And below my tail, something was getting bigger and more tender. I didn't get a good look at it, but it definitely wasn't normal. I was on the road to discover what was happening under my tail.

As I made my way on the winding, narrow road up the mountain, I heard and sensed some animal catching up with me. At first, I assumed some turkeys were out looking for mushrooms near the road, or even skunks. No way was I gonna bother them guys. I sped up my strut and didn't dare look back.

Whatever was following me was getting closer. I stopped abruptly, turned to my side, and there looking at my butt was another dog, something I hadn't seen since that day at the vet's more than three months ago. Savoring the alluring scent of his maleness, I noticed he also was rather good looking. Strong bones, a shiny wind-blown coat of mostly rusty hair. His eyes reflected the sun. His nose pointed to good days ahead, and he was so agile. A real male, if I do say so myself.

I felt giddy. My private parts were vibrating and wanted to move closer to him. We both moved closer, smelling with delight all the fertility in each other.

C'mon, I thought to myself. *You're not a human. You don't fall in love with another dog. Or do you?*

We gave each other flirty dog smiles. I think we were doing what humans called courting. I remembered that movie Sara had me watch many moons ago on the screen that talked and moved. Seems it was *Lady and the Tramp.* I fell asleep during most of it, but if I remember right, Sara had told me that the tramp and the lady dogs were in love. At the end of the movie, they had baby pups. That part I liked, because being a pup of an adoring mama was the best time in my life.

I smelled this male's ass and the thing between his back legs that seemed to be enlarging in front of me. Then, it was his turn to smell all of my special parts. The male even licked that part of me that was vibrating and seemed to be sending weird messages to my mind. Both of us let out howls, which was an infrequent voice for me.

"Have you seen the movie *Lady and the Tramp*?" I asked this most gorgeous (and maybe the only) grown male I'd ever seen.

"Nope," he answered in his Appalachian accent. "I don't watch movies. Don't even know what a movie is. Are you an indoor dog or what?"

"Sadly indoor," I answered. "Are you still wild, not tamed at all? Do you pee and poop whenever and wherever you want? Do you eat food you've caught yourself? Have you ever had dog food?"

"Just the dog food I catch, my beautiful lady. Want to make out a little?"

"Meaning?"

"You know, I lick and smell you in the places that turn me on, and you do the same. Then, we can see where it goes from there. You seem pretty young. Are you a virgin? I would wager you are."

"A virgin? What's that?"

"Usually, a female that has never been penetrated by something like this." He turned over to lay on his back, showing off his penis that was very prominent now.

"Well, I guess I am. Now, let me ask you a question." I started panting uncontrollably, like I was about to faint. "What do the words *fixing*, *spaying*, and *surgery* mean?"

"I may be a country and wild dog, but I do know you won't like the answer. So, I'll keep my mouth shut about that for now. Want to make out?"

"Nope, I have to go on until I can get the answer to my questions. That's why I'm out here today. It was nice meeting you."

"Hey, where you from, by the way? I might want to come over and see you sometime in the next few days," the handsome male winked. "I think we got some type of chemistry here 'tween us."

I tried to walk on and ignore his flirting remarks. Basically, I was entirely confused, and really didn't want to walk on. I wanted to stay with this dog, spend the day with him. Get to know him even better, maybe even do some *making out* with him.

I turned around and didn't want to walk back to him. But I did, running until I stopped abruptly right at his nose. "I might make out with you if you'll tell me what those words mean that I asked you about."

"Okay. Okay. Just for you. When a female puppy gets about your age, the humans often will do surgery to remove a special part that's inside her body. If they don't do this, you'll probably have puppies very often. And it's males like me that put the stuff in you that helps that body part make puppies. In other words, they *fix* you by *spaying* you so that you'll never have puppies."

Stunned, I stepped back and stared at the know-it-all dog. "You mean, if they don't *fix* me, I can have my own puppies someday? Why would anyone *not* want me to have pups? I want to have puppies of my own because, not long ago, I was a puppy, and it was the most wonderful experience of my life."

"Don't ask me. You know, humans control the world. But you female dogs—or bitches, as some of us call you—you have big litters. And you can birth these little pups twice a year till you die, almost. I guess the humans think they're being humane to *fix* you."

"So that's it, huh? Shouldn't I have a say about my body, about how many puppies I want to have? I gotta go home and do some thinking about this. I don't know if I should hate my owners or love them for thinking they're doing the best thing for me. If that's the case, why don't they get fixed?" I stopped and thought again. "Maybe they do get fixed. Maybe that's why they just had Sara—hmm."

"Okay, you little rebel, but can I come see you soon? I'm really attracted to you while you're in heat. It's like you glow with vitality, love, life, and fertility."

"Aw, I bet you say this to all the bitches in heat," I said. "Come on by. We're the only place on this road with a huge tree in the backyard. But I can't promise the humans will let you in where they eat and sleep. And maybe they'll have me at that damn vet's place, where they'll cut me into pieces."

"Darling, I'll be thinking of you. And remember, we males can smell your body juices miles away. I won't be sleeping tonight, because I'll be wanting to make wild, passionate love with you."

All the way home—and I really didn't want to go there—I thought of that smelly dog. Why did I forget to ask him his name? The closer I got to where Sara lived, the more scared I got. Would Mr. Gregg be at the door ready to scoop me up and take me to the vet? I certainly didn't want to be fixed. I wanted to do what bitches are made to do, have puppies over and over and over until we die.

Then, I got another thought—probably from living with humans too long. What would happen to all the pups I would birth? Would there be too many of them? Would they have enough food to eat out in the open? Would they eat all the rabbits and fish and 'possums? Would we all starve because we ate all the food running around in the woods?

I knew that some of them would die young, just like my bro Rolf did. The weaker ones wouldn't make it. Some of the stronger ones would get in fights and be killed. Some would go live with humans and not have any babies ever. Only the strongest, the smartest, and the luckiest ones would live on.

I had almost arrived at the kitchen door. Mr. Gregg's truck was in the driveway. He was probably looking in the fridge about now to decide what he should cook for dinner. I could hear the talking and moving screen entertaining Sara with some kids' movie. Would they miss me if I left for good now? I told myself I'd done my part in bringing some type of stability to the home after Mrs. Gregg's death. Sara needed to find a dog that liked to strut on a leash, to wear bright sweaters, and go to doggie spas.

But I was in heat. I had to think of my life now. I wanted to be a real dog that wasn't afraid to get dirty, to howl at night if I wanted, to make love with that sexy dog up the mountain. It truly was time to move on to taking care of Blackeye, the bitch.

Chapter 11

I hit the road running after one last panoramic view of what had been my home for the last four months. And even though I still wanted nothing to do with humans, I could almost hear Mrs. Gregg urging me on, as though her spirit wanted to experience the life of the wild creature through me.

"Okay, Mrs. Gregg, I'll show you a good time. Sorry it didn't work out 'tween me and your little girl."

I spent all of my breath running up that mountain again. I wanted to find that lover dog who had flirted with me and made me feel so alive. But it was getting dark. The moon was a sliver tonight. Either Flirty Dog would have to show up soon or I'd have to find a culvert to spend the night curled up in.

Then, there was the little matter of food. *None tonight*, I thought. I would hunt tomorrow to stop my stomach from growling.

After about an hour I realized I was truly alone in the big wild world. No one was going to come and save me—as though I wanted to be saved. Not me, I was tough, and I would prove it every day for the rest of my life. I started to shift my gaze now to the ditches along the road, searching for a place where I could sleep the entire night in peace. No comfy cushion anymore. No heat pump that clicked on when the room got chilly or hot. I began to hear the night life, probably little bugs looking for mates. All I was looking for was a place to lay my head for the night.

My nose could pick up on scents that would lead me to the place I needed to be. It picked up on a familiar smell from this afternoon. Was it the grass or the nearby spring? Nope. This was the smell of a living being with hot blood pumping through his veins. And it wasn't Mr. Gregg. This smell came from a canine like me. Maybe Flirty Dog had found me—or, more accurately, rescued me. I heard barking now. Definitely he was on my trail.

I sped up. I wanted to play hard to get, to pretend I didn't give a lick about him. He sped up behind me. He definitely was interested in the chase. But the faster I ran, he ran even faster, just like I wanted him to do. Then, I became poor little worn-out me, a bitch in distress. I stopped, laid down on the chilling road, and panted to catch my breath.

And there he was, at my side, licking my face. He looked dangerous at night, being so much bigger than me. I wondered how old he really was. Was he old enough to be my father or grandfather? Was he any of these? I had never met my father. The only father I knew was Mr. Gregg, but humans don't count.

"You don't belong out here at this time of night," he scolded me after his tongue became dry from licking me.

"Oh, I didn't tell you?" I teased back. "I've decided to run away. I want to be a wild dog, do all the stuff wild animals do. I'm not a human, and I don't want to follow humans' rules in humans' homes. Nope, a dog's life is for me, beginning tonight. You know where I can stay for the night?"

"Well, let me see." He grew quiet as he covered his eyes with both front paws. "I don't know of anything that would be up to the quality you deserve." He looked into my eyes. "Why'd you ditch a good thing, that fancy place you were living in?"

"Duh, I just told you. I don't belong there anymore. I'm made for the wild, with the wolves, the foxes, and the coyotes. Do you think I'm a weakling city-type dog that belongs on a leash being dragged along city sidewalks, getting my nails trimmed, wearing doggie sweaters? That's not me."

"Well, you smell pretty clean to me, like that stuff humans wash their hair with."

"You mean shampoo?"

"If you say so. I've never been invited into a human's place. What do they do with all their pee and shit? I never see them squatting outside. But I have seen some male humans pulling their wieners out to see how far out they can squirt their pee."

I certainly could answer that. "They have special rooms in their places called bathrooms. They sit on something like a big deep bowl and maybe read the newspaper or do a puzzle while they poop. When they're all done, they wipe their butt, throw the paper into the bowl with the poop, push down a handle on the bowl, and everything swishes down under the floor. If they want, sometimes they'll spray this stinky, cloudy stuff from a can to cover up that nice-smelling shit. Then, they wash their hands. All done."

"Hmm, sounds kind of weird. And they get smelly stuff to change the smell of the poop? What do you eat when you're with the humans? Does the man or the mama bring in ducks or rats or coons they find out in the woods?"

"Not that I've noticed. They go to a store. Surely, you've found a few dumpsters that you can find food in. They're usually in the back of stores where they put old food that can't be sold."

"Oh, really. That's where I've just come from. Want some ribs? They have some kind of smokey, sticky stuff on 'em, but by the time you reach the bones, they're not bad."

"So, you don't hunt like a real manly dog? You don't chase rabbits or catch fish?"

"Aw, sometimes. But in case you didn't notice, I'm a little older than you. You're still a child and a virgin. I've, let's say, been around."

"How many puppies have you helped create?" I asked.

"Oh, I don't know. Never counted 'em. A dog's job is done as soon as he breeds the bitch. Then, what follows is all up to her."

"Is that the way things are out in the wild? You males don't help the mama out at all?"

"Well, dogs got other things to do, like eating and occasionally breeding more bitches. When they want it, they gotta have it now. And there's lots of competition out there. The younger guys are getting tougher and tougher, you know. Older males gotta keep their stamina up to beat off these younger twirps. And then there are the packs. Have you ever been chased or gnawed on by a pack of dogs?"

I shook my head no. I felt my eyes getting as big as eggs. I was scared. "Do packs of dogs gang up on us bitches, and have their turns with us?"

"Not quite, but won't say it never happens. What usually happens is there is this so-called alpha dog, kind of like a bull in a herd of cattle, or a stallion leading a herd of mares. In a pack, the other male dogs let the alpha dog do the breeding. Of course, eventually the alpha wears out and another male rises up to take his place."

"Why are you a loner? Did you ever join a pack?"

"Nope, you might call me a *lone wolf*."

"Are you telling me you're not even a dog, but a wolf?"

"Could be."

"I'm scared of wolves."

"Now, come on. Do I look scary? Look at me. I don't go out and attack livestock or even chickens. I find getting my food from dumpsters works wonders for me. In my early days, I would kill a few rabbits or rats, but all that hair got caught 'tween my teeth and tasted like dirt. Am I not wild enough for you?"

"I don't know. All of this is so new to me. I don't know what I want or need. Do you think I should go home and grow up more?"

"Wouldn't be caught dead living where humans live. I need to be free out here with the wind, the rain, and the snow. They're my relatives, you know."

"Can I sleep with you tonight?" I asked. It didn't look like he would ever get around to asking me.

"I guess."

"You'll leave me alone?"

"You mean, will I mount you?"

"Yeah."

"I think I'll wait awhile. Experience tells me that since you seem to be pretty dumb about stuff like bitches in heat, you're not quite ripe for picking. But I'll respect your wishes if you promise me that I'll be first in line for the pleasure of your company when you're ripe for being mounted."

"Doggone, you drive a hard bargain on rent. But I do kind of love you. Do you think you love me?"

"That's more of a word that humans use to cover up their desire to do some mounting. To be truthful, being a wolf, I don't know if I love you or not. But I sure want to be with you until we can do our thing as a twosome."

I didn't know how to interpret all of this wolf's talk. Had I become humanized or too civilized? Would I be content out here in the wild? I had a lot of growing up to do—and thinking. Golly, my first hook-up could—would—be with a wolf.

I smiled.

Chapter 12

I've since learned the breed of this wolf in North Carolina is called a *red wolf,* and most have moved to the eastern part of the state. How this guy ended up here in the mountains, I didn't know. Nevertheless, this flirty guy led me farther up the road to an old lean-to, which seemed to have been abandoned decades ago. He went in first, turned around, and motioned me in after him. He gave me some bones to gnaw on. I pretended they were tender meat, but the bones felt so good on my maturing teeth. As a matter of fact, I actually fell asleep gnawing on a rib from the dumpster.

During the night, my new wolf friend moved closer to me to keep both of us warm and snug. I awoke when a tiny mouse scooted past me, tickling my front paws in the process. I jumped, since by now I had forgotten the mice that used to play with us puppies in the barn. The wolf growled in his sleep until I started licking his paws. He reminded me of a mild-mannered giant.

I found the bone I had gnawed on last night and started in on it again. This time, my insides told me they wanted more than little bits of bone. I decided to step outside the lean-to and breathe in the fresh forest air. I looked around for sources for food. I saw birds in the air. Couldn't jump high enough to catch one of 'em. I saw a few more tender little mice, which could make good appetizers. I actually was able to catch one with my mouth. A couple bites, and I swallowed it. I felt it tickle my throat as it protested going down my throat on the way to my stomach. I felt a little cruel securing my first meal from a helpless, innocent mouse. But a dog's gotta eat.

As I dealt with my guilt baggage, the wolf snuck up on me from behind. He took a quick sniff and smiled a big bad wolf smile. "Coming along well there, girl. Someday, you'll be a mama with darling wolf pups nibbling on your nipples. I can tell you right now that you'll be a great little nurturing mama. And I can be their daddy, passing on my great looks, strength, and fierceness."

"Well, aren't you full of it this morning?" I asked.

"You want to make out?" the flirty wolf asked.

"When I feel you near and smell your strong wolf juices, I get turned on, Mr. Wolf. By the way, what is your name? Do you have one?"

"Depends on whether you like me or hate me. Those who hate me call me Bastard. Those who like and respect me call me Super Bastard, or Super for short."

"Ha ha, aren't you the funny one," I joked back.

"I'm still about making our own little pack, you and me. You'll really love me, girl."

If I were a human, I would have been blushing. Seems I was growing up too fast. I was attracted to this wolf, but was I ready to be all grown up so soon? It seemed like yesterday (and I guess it was yesterday, wasn't it?) that I was being led around by a little girl younger than Super. Now, I seemed to be with the biggies, and they weren't playing around. This was serious stuff. Super was sticking with me because he intended to breed me. Then, I would get fat and give birth to a litter of wolfdogs. Would that hurt? Would they be big and mean like wolves or sweet and cuddly like me and my brothers?

I needed some advice. I couldn't go home and talk to anyone there. Mrs. Gregg wasn't speaking to my soul when I really needed it. Maybe I needed to go farther out in the forest and hear the voices of my ancestors.

"Super, I need to go away on a vision quest," I said. "I'm feeling confused right now. Things are changing too fast for me. Here I am now, about to go into real heat. I feel like I'm still just a puppy. I'm used to humans—and not a horny wolf—taking care of me and feeding me. Am I ready to be a grown-up dog now? Am I rushing things? I think maybe my body wants to give me the answers I need to listen to."

"Go, baby. You'll be back. I know you better than you know yourself. Tell you the truth, I felt the same way when I was transitioning from a wolf pup to a full-grown bitch charmer like I am now. I'll be here when you get back. Here, wait. I'll send some food with you, baby."

How thoughtful of him, I thought. Maybe he was the right fellow. I hoped to find out.

In no time at all, Super was back with a few more ribs with some meat still on them. He had them in a bag that I could carry in my mouth. With the baby mouse still rolling around in my tummy, I trudged on into the deep forest. I hoped I could walk in as a scared pup and walk out as a mature bitch ready to do my duty for the future of canines on earth.

Chapter 13

I didn't realize how naive I was until I found myself alone in the mysterious forest that had no end. In the small woods near the humans' home, I'd gravitated to another huge oak tree, even taller than the one at the Gregg family's home. In this forest, ragged rocks poked out of the ground. Huge birds kept watch from above. Millions of centipedes wiggled under my paws. All was darker in the forest, even in the heat of the day. I didn't look forward to the night ahead when there would be pitch darkness.

I finally found a gigantic rock that jutted out over a deep drop below. Here the sun shone, and the blue sky hypnotized my mind. I decided to sit for a long time while my body adjusted to my new identity. Meanwhile, my butt was continuing to swell and seemed to be bleeding a little. This part of me was speaking out loud and demanding. My body was ready to mate. I didn't have to mate. I could get fixed, like the Greggs had wanted. I would sleep through the operation and soon recover. I would never have to think about horny dogs again in my life. I could get fat and sassy, fetch balls, and beg for more. I could be groomed and sent to doggie spas and play with other dogs in dog parks. I could put on a proud strut, wear a diamond-studded collar, and walk up and down a boardwalk at the beach, along trails in the park, or be pushed in a doggie stroller past boutiques in Hightown among other like-minded, well-behaved dogs with no puppies.

And that's what baffled me the most. No puppies. No grown-up dog responsibilities. I would be a walking toy for humans. I would die as a toy. My role as cheerleader to boost humans' self-esteem would be my reason to exist. My life would be purposeless regarding other dogs. Everything I would eventually know would be what humans taught me. I would have a chip put under the skin of my ear so I could always be returned to my owners, whether I liked them or not.

My choices were complicated. The difference was a life of comfort and selling out, or a life of giving birth and nurturing new life. If I chose life in the wild, all would not be idyllic. My mates and puppies would abandon me to loneliness between weanings and coming into heat. I would travail through burdensome pregnancies, painful births, and some dying puppies, too weak to survive. Could I really adjust to being wild?

Humans or countless puppies. These were the choices. Most dogs would choose humans. I had to decide if I was ready to do the other.

Chapter 14

With that last thought, I was ready to stop thinking for a while. The June sun warmed me like a pup in a womb. I wanted to crawl back into Mama for just a few hours—well, maybe for a few weeks. I knew I was too big to do that. Old enough now to soon become a mama myself. But for the time being, the sun could warm me like a mama. I closed my eyes and formed my body into a ball as much as possible. I thought of nothing. My mind was gone.

Now, everything was experiential. I didn't wonder why or how, where or when. I just was. I was being combed. My hair was untangled and felt so smooth when my tiny paws slid over it. I smelled fresh doggie milk stored in full doggie tits. I was hungry and then satisfied. Straw tickled me from my nose to my hiney. I moved closer to my mama and made little yippie sounds. I looked into her loving, dark eyes. I heard the pigeons cooing above me and squeaks of baby mice over in a nearby bale of hay. I opened my eyes and noticed a bright ray of sun squeezing through the slats of the barn's walls. Then, there were little fuzzy things floating in that ray, always floating, never landing. Not a care in the world. All the earth was in this barn. I sometimes heard the rain plopping down on the roof above me or saw the lightning flashing during the dark parts of the day. But at this very moment, the sun was kind. She was my mama, watching over me and warming me.

In other words, I was napping and dreaming. I escaped until the sun decided it was time to set herself. My little perch above the canyon below was losing its warmth and turning cold. I hadn't looked for a place to gnaw on my bones before falling asleep again. I had to hurry. Time for pleasure and meditating on roads ahead had to surrender their importance so I could sleep in safety tonight.

I tuned into my senses, especially my smell and hearing. I moved off the ledge and scampered down closer to the veins of the earth. I smelled other animals, and I heard tiny feet and birds calling for their mates and babies to come home. I was drawn to the old growth of the forest. The tall elms and poplars beckoned me into their presence. I obeyed. And there in the bedroom of the ancestor trees were huge trunks of trees which had fallen to the ground, leaving gigantic holes where their roots had once supported bulky trunks and crooked limbs. This was where I would sleep tonight as my body and soul sorted through my hopes and desires, my identity and boundaries.

I settled into the clumpy dirt, where some stubborn roots remained. I asked them why they stayed put when most of the rest of the tree had collapsed. One said he hadn't been invited to leave with the rest of the tree. Another said she had nutrition where she was, and one day she would sprout some leaves and start a sibling tree.

Oh, this life in the forest! It was like the middle of a big city but made up of diverse plant life instead of buildings and humans. No stop lights or speed limits. Only a world gone wild with berries, nuts, mushrooms, medicinals, briars, and poison ivy. Little puddles of muddy water were looking for a stream so their waters could someday visit the ocean. I asked if I could come along. But I was turned down because I didn't know how to swim yet.

There I was, marveling at my new habitat and my new neighbors, when a huge black bear came along. I hoped she wouldn't notice me, but being a white dog, it was hard to blend in. Our eyes actually met, but that was it. She crawled into a hollow log, which I wished I had seen myself. But it was all for the better that I'd ended up where I was. If she had seen me in her domicile, she might have eaten me or seriously injured me.

I continued to quietly gnaw on the spicy ribs Super had insisted I carry with me. My jaws tired from the workout, and my face was like Sara's face when she had one of those suckers in her mouth too long. The thought of Sara not having her mama there to tuck her in made me sad. This would be her second night without me. I could almost hear her sobbing on her pillow, worrying that I, too, was probably dead, killed by a black bear in the forest.

And after Sara, I saw some fog, but in the shape of a woman about the same height as Mrs. Gregg. Was she going to tell me to get home right now? Nope.

"I'm following you, my sweet little puppy," I heard her say. "I see you're turning into a beautiful bitch now. I know you're confused and scared. I probably am somewhat responsible for you leaving my house. I encouraged you to follow your dream into the wild. I envied your passion to be rid of human ways and civilization, or at least what we call civilization. I sometimes wonder what values we live by these days."

"Why are you out here tonight? Why are you following me?" I blinked to be sure she was really there beside me.

"Didn't I tell you I would look in on you now and then? Remember, I settled on what I thought was expected of me. I married a successful man and bore a beautiful child. I thought I would always be happy as a result of these decisions. But I wasn't. Then, you came along. You know I didn't want you, right? But you opened a window in my life that I had thought would always remain closed."

"Is that why you killed yourself? You're saying it was my fault? No! I won't take the blame!" I was about ready to attack her.

"No, it wasn't your fault, you silly dog. I just didn't see a way out of my family's expectations. I blew it. I should have talked it out before escaping into death. But now, I can't go back. So, here I am with you. I want you to be free to do what your passions say you must do."

Now, I could speak frankly with her. "I think you did the cowardly thing, deserting those you loved by killing yourself. Why don't you go back to them now and tell them you're sorry?" I urged.

"Can't do. They have to be in the moment when they'll be most receptive. That day will come, and when it does, I'll do just that. Tonight, you're receptive to my visit. I heard you earlier wondering how you would spend your life. Seems you're still confused. You're entering a time of life when your hormones—materials pulsating through you that control feelings in your mind and body—are changing. Now, you're about in heat. Heck, you already are. But this is your first experience with this emotional and physical miracle that is your body. You're still young. Even if that wolf you are attracted to mates with you, nothing may happen. Or if it does, you may give birth to only one pup, and it may be sickly. I'm not telling you to worry about these things. I just want you to go ahead with your eyes open for both good results and possible disappointments that follow."

"How do you know anything about us dogs?" I questioned. "You're a human. I don't know much about you humans, and I don't expect you to obsess about us dogs' lives."

"Hey, can you keep it down over there?" the bear growled, scaring me almost to death.

"Okay!" I yelled back. I then told Mrs. Gregg to leave. She'd spoken her piece.

"Remember, I'm always around when you feel receptive," she said as she began to fade away. "And also, as far as Super goes, if you feel drawn to him, join with him. If you don't, then leave."

"That woman!" I growled. Here I'd thought I had rid myself of humans and their baggage. Now, one was following me around as a ghost.

Oh well, maybe I needed to hear her advice, even if it was coming from a human. After all, I was on a quest. And strange things happen when you open yourself up in pursuit of wisdom. Okay, I would think about her words.

Chapter 15

My vision quest was beginning to be full of visions and too many questions without many answers.

The bones were about chewed apart, and I was famished. Would I again have to eat a small varmint to quiet my stomach? Oh, life was so much easier with the humans. All I had to do was look at an empty bowl and transfer that look to a human, and out would come a can. They'd lift the little circle thing at the top, and off would come a lid. Then, I would gobble the whole contents up in a few gulps.

Was I trying to talk myself into going back to them now, or was I only being realistic? I surely could get used to this life if I really wanted to. I could sleep in the cold, couldn't I? Could I go dumpster diving with Super? Could I deliver babies all by myself? Would the humans allow me to come back when I was big and fat with puppies inside me so they wouldn't freeze out in the wild? I decided to call that Plan B. For now, it was time to hunt.

I surely had a little of the hunter in my bloodline, I told myself, as I snuck behind a big rock to watch some other animal smaller than me scamper by. It was still officially spring. Maybe a mama rabbit would ramble by with her little bunnies trotting along with her. I could surely catch a small, fuzzy bunny and make a meal of it.

Then, I put myself in the place of the mama rabbit. Shame on me for even considering such a thing. So, there I stood, poised to leap out at a creature to eat. Then, I saw it. A turtle. They were slow, and if I was able to somehow tear open the soft flesh underneath the top shell, I would be in for a satisfying meal.

I leapt forward and practically landed on top of the little guy. He looked up at me with pleading eyes. I closed mine, tipped him over, and started to tear his underbelly apart. All the while I was doing this, I felt like a murderer. But it was too late. The damage was done. The turtle suddenly stopped trying to get away. Its eyes stopped pleading. And I was eating faster and faster, as though if I slowed down, my guilt would boil over and I would be sick of what I was doing and hate myself. It did taste good, however. But that's dogs for you. Or maybe hunger will do that to every animal.

I ate as much as I could and dragged the rest of the turtle back to the tree hole. I covered it with leaves and resumed my quest in the forest. I studied the plants and ate some of the grass I found here and there for digestive purposes. I spun around in circles and nursed the swelling flesh around my butt. I could taste the oozing body fluids as I licked.

This being in heat thing was beginning to drive me crazy. Even though Mrs. Gregg had warned me last night that this season could be a disappointing one for me, my body didn't get the message. It wanted a stud to penetrate it, like it was a balloon too full of air. To be penetrated would release some of that tension, perhaps. Then, I could go on with life. Maybe a pregnancy would result. Maybe not. But living with this nervousness and yearning was overwhelming. Nature was demanding, it seemed. I knew that it was time for my quest to end and for me to go back to see Super.

Just admitting that I wasn't going to fight my desires and drives any longer but instead flow with them wherever they led me seemed to help. It even gave me more energy and heightened my instincts, like I was following a string that would eventually lead me back to Super and mad, insane lovemaking until these urges went away.

Chapter 16

I was on fire with passion for Super. I wasn't sure he was really as charming as I was imagining, but he had taken an interest in me, and that was all I needed.

I stopped to rest as the forest began to change from a thick, fertile maze to a cultured field of serene trees and berry bushes with lots of emerging grasses and weeds.

I decided to catch my breath underneath an old willow with limbs that seemed to invite me in. As my breathing slowed down, I had a chance to definitely decide if I would mate with Super. I was listening to the ripples of a creek rushing toward the river when I noticed an animal about my size running toward me.

At first, I couldn't identify what this animal was. It ran like a happy dog, but it was so lean and fast. My curiosity heightened. Since it was galloping my way, I continued to sit under the willow and watch. No way was I to know what this was. I had never seen such an animal. Tiny head, long legs and full of grace. Since it was so fast, I didn't have to stare for long.

It appeared that this animal was the dog version of a racehorse with a dog's body. He stopped when he got to me. Of course, we greeted each other with the regular smelling of our coats, behinds, and underbellies. I was impressed, and he seemed to be impressed with me, too.

"Why are you in such a hurry?" I asked this athletic dog.

"Surely you can guess. I got a whiff of you down at the Winters' farm over there on that hill." Of course, he pointed with his extremely pointed nose.

"Well, I'm Blackeye. Sorry my being in heat interrupted your day. Your family must be worried about you. You'd better get home."

"Aw, couldn't do that. Not right away anyway. You look sorta young. This your first *in season?*"

"I guess so. It's all so confusing. I'm not ready to mate yet, however. I was born in the cold months. I'm barely out of the puppy stage. I don't know why I had to go into heat so young."

"Aw, just nature. She's what controls what happens to you. I think ol' Mama Nature can't wait for you to have some puppies. That's why she sent me to search for you. Glad to make your acquaintance. I'm Racer. I guess you can figure out how I got named."

"Yep, you seem to be real fast, for sure. What breed do the humans call you?"

"I've heard 'em say greyhound. Ever hear of us? Purebred, too. Impressed?"

"I'm certainly not one of those. Just a mixture of whatever interested my mama, I guess."

Racer couldn't take his eyes off my butt, which was considerably more swollen and rosier today. "Doesn't seem your mama was the choosy type. But you turned out fine."

I was flattered by the compliment. Still, I wanted to see Super. I was beginning to think that Racer had his name in the pot to make passionate love as well. This life in the wild as a bitch in heat was overwhelming for a young female barely out of puppyhood.

You know, we dogs don't really have strict morals. I was to find out later that I could have multiple lovers or studs. But I think some of the humans' morals had rubbed off onto me. I wanted a mate who wouldn't breed me and leave. I wanted someone who would be attracted to me when I wasn't in heat. Was that asking for too much?

"Well, nice meeting you, Racer," I said as I emerged from under the willow. I kind of wanted him to beg me to stay. And I kinda wanted to stay. But I walked on.

Before I knew it, he was at my rear, smelling me as I walked. I was flattered, but I also knew he was simply following his instincts. He didn't love me for my great personality or beauty. No, he wanted a part of me. He wanted to spread his DNA by using me.

"Hey, I know how to fish," he said. "I bet you're hungry, ain't cha? I am. Let me catch you a bass or catfish. Then, we can talk over lunch. In your condition, you need to keep your health up."

I was kinda hungry, and Racer was sure cute. After all, we were just dogs doing what came naturally. We were a friendly species, folks often said. So, why not?

"Hmm. That does sound appetizing. Could be fun too. Let me see how you fish so I can take up the practice out here in the wild."

I followed him over to the creek. He drooled over me as I cautiously made my way down to the water. The path was slippery, so I had to watch my step. He rubbed my nose with his when I finally made it. He was a romantic fellow, I had to admit.

"So, we kinda stand at attention and watch the water flow away from us," he said. "Ya gotta adjust your eyes to see into the water. Fish, you know, move fast, and they kind of blend in with the water. It's easy to miss 'em." Racer put his long front leg around my small shoulders.

All of a sudden, he drew it back and dove into the water. He came back up with a trout clenched between his jaws. He tore a piece of meat off and gave it to me. I took a few nibbles. I'd never had fish that didn't come out of a can before. This one had scales, and they tickled my throat as I swallowed my small bites.

He looked deeply in my eyes. "You like it, don't you? Can't get fresher meat anywhere. Here, take another bite. You need to keep your strength up if you're gonna bear my pups someday."

"Hey, I never, never said I would bear your pups. You're a lot bigger than me. I don't see how I could bear such big puppies."

"Aw, no problem. I've bred lots of bitches much smaller than you. Everything went fine. Don't worry. Baby pups have soft bones that allow them to just sail out of you like a hiccup. You'll see."

"So, this is why you took me fishing, so I'd melt under your mount?" I asked. "Then, you'd leave to go back to the Winters, and I'd never see you again. I gotta get used to this idea."

"Well, little woman, that's how we live out here in the wild. If it's not your bag, go home to the humans who rescued you. Let them turn you into another human with four legs." He started to dog-laugh at his little joke.

I didn't laugh, but I did start thinking again. I imagined walking on a leash, having to hold my pee and poop until someone took me outside. I thought about what it would be like to be fixed, to never desire mates. To live to eat canned food, to pretend that I was protecting the humans. To never have puppies. But also, to never freeze to death during the cold months.

"Whatcha doing, little lady?"

"Hey, maybe you saw *Lady and the Tramp*. Have you seen that movie? It was animated, but another version had real dogs."

"Nope, didn't see it," Racer said. "Sorry. But I got an idea where you're going with this. It may look like I have a small brain, but it's not. Just more condensed. Lots of mass up there above my eyes and below my ears."

"Okay, tell me where you're going with this," I demanded.

"Those humans got 'em, too. That's why I know what's going on here. They're trying to brainwash you. Don't let 'em do it."

"But you, you have the best of both worlds," I quipped. "The Winters seem to let you live a life of freedom in the wild. But you can go home at night and eat their food and sleep in their warm house on their soft cushions. Plus, they don't want to fix you," I countered.

"Well, it might be a little like that, but I'm still a stud. Can't you see that I am? I want to make mad and passionate love with you. Now, you know where I live. Once you get heavy with my puppies, come visit me. Maybe they'll want the pick of the litter."

I thought he was joking. He didn't want me scratching on his door in the middle of the night and asking to be let in. Or was he serious?

"You mean what you just said?" I asked.

"Sure. You just ran away, right?"

"Yeah. So what?"

"Summer's just beginning. Enjoy your summer in the wild. Grow up. And grow my puppies. When you feel the pains of birth coming on, drop in and see me. We'll see what we can do. I'll wipe your brow if you want. Or help you breathe."

This proposal was getting interesting. "Okay," I said hesitantly. "Do I go home with you now and meet your people?"

"No, you don't do that. You haven't even mated with me yet. Ask me after it's all over, and I'll let you know. For now, let's finish this trout off."

Chapter 17

We picked the flesh of the fish down to the bare bones. Then, we licked the bones clean.

"Want another?" Racer asked.

"No, I don't think so, but thank you for giving me fishing instructions. You want to mate now? Remember, I'm a young virgin. I don't even know if I'm fertile yet. I'm scared out of my wits right now."

"Don't worry, pretty girl. I'll be gentle. I'm experienced at this kind of thing. Believe me, it's an experience you'll treasure the rest of your life. You ready?"

Racer had convinced me. I was ready, but still scared. This was the biggest moment of my life. I told myself to just smell his fabulous parts and relax. The fear would go away as we got with the program.

Oh, he smelled so good. I was mesmerized. My brain seemed to be fogging up and the rest of my body was taking over. I looked into his adorable eyes. And I could see he was about his business. His eyes were glazed with pure passion. He was the king, and I was his subject.

Instinct took over, even for me. I backed into his face. He licked my butt and then he mounted me. At first, I thought he would crush me, but like he had promised, he was gentle. My entire behind was vibrating and tingling like I had left earth and was in some type of pleasure chamber. His most intimate part slipped into me, and I sighed. But the real joy was just beginning. He thrust his part into me over and over, and each time I felt the thrust, my body wanted to hold it forever. But there was to be more. How could a bitch ever feel anything so exhilarating?

I wondered why he stopped. My body told me that he was releasing the little droplets that would mingle with mine eventually to make a litter.

When we both had reached the midst of dog heaven and wanted to rest in its glow, something in me encased his private part and wouldn't release it. No matter what position he or I moved into, he stayed in me. For a long time, his rear was facing mine. Our faces were facing out at the world. I know, I'm just a dog and am ruled by instinct only. But wow, I'll take instinct any day.

I finally released him. It was over. It was too late to back out now. As our eyes met after the mating, I asked if I could go see where he lived.

He said, "Not now, beautiful. I'll get in touch maybe in a couple months. Nice knowing you."

And that was the end of my first mating experience. Lots to think about, for sure.

Chapter 18

Here I was, alone again. Yes, I had found a life out in the wild. But all wasn't as perfect as I had naively assumed. Don't tell anyone, but I was lonely.

And this was just minutes after I had mated with this handsome greyhound named Racer. He had caught a fish for me and had promised to be gentle. The mating experience was amazing. I guess I'd thought I had won his heart, but instead I only won his little poking part. Now, look. Where was he? Nowhere to be seen. He had left me high and very dry. I wanted to throw up every fiber of trout I had eaten and plaster it on his beautiful face.

Here I was acting more like a human than a simple bitch, put out here to fulfill males' desires. I was able to analyze the whole deal. My role was to go into heat, mate, gestate a litter of puppies, feed them, and then start all over. In the dog world, there is no social equity. No, we bitches fulfill our roles like the studs do. Everyone's happy, and the dog population goes up like Mama Nature likes to see.

Heck, this was probably just the post-coupling blues. I had enjoyed the episode immensely and expected the feeling to last forever. I should have known better. Maybe in a couple months I'd deliver my first litter of puppies. Then, like my mama, I'd be happy again. I would be such a perfect mama and would develop close relationships with my pups. And they would love me forever, unlike Racer, who just walked away with his chest pumped out like a big rock showing his male prowess.

Knowing that my pups would develop inside me within two moons, I knew I had no time to feel sorry for myself. If the breeding took, these little pups were now forming from practically nothing inside my body. In a few weeks, I would feel some movement and I'd get that glow of new mothers. I would proudly walk around in the woods showing off my pregnancy, my fertility.

But for now, it was time for a nap. No use worrying about the future. My main job was to get out of the way of the natural development of pups in my belly. To honor that, I lay down again under the willow tree, falling fast asleep under its protective branches.

I could say that I had a dream that showed me my future as an important bitch in the dog society here in Western North Carolina. But to tell the truth, my mind seemed to be an empty bowl. Was it too resting from my encounter with Racer and readying itself for a stressful time ahead? All I know is that I slept soundly, like I was a contented puppy myself. No brain, no hunger, no hopes, hurts, or fears. My body shifted into the task of incubating puppies. Maybe.

I was also aware that nothing might come of this mating. I had to be ready for the disappointment of discovering this and waiting for another season to try again. When I awoke, I made a big doggie yawn and looked around me. The sun was setting. What was the use of looking for Super? My fascination with him was over. I made a nice little place for myself under the willow tree. I would watch the sunset and call it a night.

Just as I was about to doze off, I felt another nose on my cheek. Had Racer come back? I knew he really needed me! I had known that all the time. But it wasn't Racer. Super was at my side.

"Worried about you, kid," he said, as I tried to hide my surprise. "Is your quest over? Tell me all about it."

All about it? Should I tell Super that I had found another and that he had already mated with me? Maybe he even knew Racer. I had to be selective in what I told the flirty wolf.

"I guess my quest is over. Anyway, I ended up here today and was too tired to go all the way back to where I left you. To tell the truth, I had a somewhat quality quest. The forest gave me lots of opportunities to think and to figure out who I was and what my purpose was out here in the wild. Seems the more I thought about it, the more confused I got, so I started back this afternoon. How have you been?"

"I saw the little girl and her father, I assume, out looking for you," he said. "I hid in the blackberry bushes. I did hear her crying. Her father was trying to console her by saying they would get another puppy. But she insisted no other puppy would do. You two had a special bond. It was quite sad, and usually I don't let human drama bother me."

"Aw, she'll get over it. She cries about the most mundane stuff, like a toy teacup breaking or her mommy dying." Had I really just said that? "I mean, she's going through growing pains. She's got a good dad. Don't worry."

But I was worried. And feeling guilty. That little girl was missing me. She loved me. These males in my life. They were just using me. Of course, she wanted to use me in another way—as her plaything, her pillow, her pal. Nope. I wouldn't fall for that. I was a different dog now. I now had puppies inside me. They were more important than a little human. I was sure they still intended to fix me, whether I had pups in me or not.

"I won't go back," I insisted. "You know, on my quest, the spirit of that girl's mother appeared to me, and basically, she encouraged me to stay with the journey I'm on now."

"Well, good. Glad we got that out of the way. Are you ready to mate yet?"

I couldn't answer right away. What? Mate again? Of course, Super didn't know about what had happened to me just a few hours ago.

"Not tonight, Super. Hey, I was thinking—how many times can a bitch expect to be mounted when she's in heat? I thought once would do it."

"Aw, you're so lucky. You can be mounted many, many times as long as you stay in heat, and that usually lasts—hmm, let me see—maybe up to forty days. You up for that?"

I started to walk around Super and smell the exciting chemicals coming from his sweaty body. He smelled so sweet and sexy. I shook my head to bring me back to sanity again.

"I know that look on your face," Super nudged me. "You think I'm tantalizing, don't you? You want me in the worst way."

"I can live with or without you. You know I'm the one who decides if I'm ready, right? You are going to have to get on your hind legs and beg first."

"Oh, so you think since you're flowering, gorgeous, and the only female in heat in these parts that you can make me beg, huh?"

"Yup, that's kinda what I'm saying. Plus, you know, I might just want to go back to live with that little girl, have them get me an abor—"

"An abortion? Is that what you were going to say?" Super asked. "Did you let some other male get to you before me, after I let you go on that quest? Of all the—"

I nudged closer to Super and smiled.

"And Super, it was so-o-o good." I put that smile into my eyes as Super's tail sunk between his two back legs. "But that doesn't mean I don't want you, too. Well, I want all you boys in the neighborhood. I want you all to line up and take your turns. I'll mate with the ones I want and kick the ones I don't want out of my Garden of Paradise. Because I hold the cards, man. And you just beg."

I couldn't believe what was coming out of my mouth. Was that me speaking to Super? I hadn't rehearsed this or anything. The thought hadn't even passed my mind. Maybe Mrs. Gregg was possessing me. Perhaps, she knew more about the laws of the wild than I did.

"You're kinda right, Blackeye," Super said. "You are the most desired jewel in this area right now. It's entirely up to you who you mate with. We males, if we were human now, would be bringing you flowers and chocolates, snuggling with you, whispering sweet words in your cute little ears. But one day, your season will be over. And no matter how much you begged for attention, we wouldn't give a sniff to your scent. You would be finished flesh. If and when you gave birth to a litter, that papa dog you mated with could try to kill them, so you'd come into heat sooner, and he could spread his seed in you again before you had a chance to recover. Males will always be interested in impregnating you when you're in season, because that's who we are and what we do. We are controlled by something humans call the law of the wild."

He intended to burst my bubble, and he did a pretty good job of it.

I tried to get my snottiness back and tell him to leave, but instead I got off my high horse and said, "Okay, I get it. I'll stay in my place, and you stay in your place, and maybe we'll be nice to each other again."

"Makes sense," Super said. "But I gotta tell you one more thing. You know I'm a wolf, don't you?"

"I think you told me that. At least part wolf, right?"

"No, I'm all wolf. That's why I'm not in a pack with the other wild dogs out here. They don't like me, and I don't like them. But one thing we wolves have over the dogs is that we stay with our bitch after we mate. Dogs don't. They're in it for the fun of it."

I didn't say anything, but this was what I had wanted to hear. I could feel my eyes water as I thought of Super as a real mate, staying with me for the rest of my life, caring for me and loving my puppies, if they were meant to exist.

"You're not shittin' me, are you, Super?"

"As long as you cling to me, I'll cling to you," he said. "But that doesn't mean I've not had other bitches in my life. C'mon, you know I've been around the block a few times. It's just that some of my bitches died or got killed. Some left me for other wolves or made the mistake of aligning themselves with the better-looking dogs out here."

"Well, I think you're kind of cute," I flirtatiously uttered. "Would you like to smell me some more and make out?"

"I'd be honored, my love," Super answered.

"Well then, I'm ready whenever you are."

I slowly edged over and surveyed his entire muscular body. I let out a howl, lifting my nose to the heavens. As I moved on in, I could see his muscles tightening. Of course, he was giving me lots of tender loving smells and looks as well. I began to realize how lucky I was that this real canine, from which dogs evolved, found me, a dog myself, to be desirable. And he wanted me to stay with him, and I wanted to stay with him, till death would we part.

I, the hopeless romantic, backed into his front paws, and Super took it from there, letting out a ferocious howl. An exquisite pairing. That was how I would describe my experience with Super. Love and sex were hot stuff. I was enjoying my bitchiness. And I didn't care if Racer saw me or not.

Love would conquer all for this *Lady and the Tramp*.

Chapter 19

So here I was now, the better half of the Super coupling. I figured I gotta be pregnant because I wanted a partner who would be proud of his offspring. I did my best to not even think of Racer anymore. If I did think of him by accident, I considered him to have been an indiscretion. He'd seduced me, an innocent young bitch who didn't know any better.

I was determined to live as a wild dog for the rest of my life. And that life would be in partnership with Super. We would be the alpha male and female. Super claimed he wasn't part of a pack. What happened, I don't know. Perhaps he was exiled from the pack, or maybe he left because another alpha male got the alpha female. He probably didn't go for being a "worker," the hunter who brought home choice prey for the alpha, his mate and cubs, but who would let the others in the pack fight over the leftovers. Thus, his choice was to go solo.

No matter what the reason, we were now a lone wolf pair of alphas. Maybe one day we'd start our own pack, like a kingdom in the wild, with me the *luna* and Super the *alpha*. I was a lovesick, reckless bitch who also liked to daydream.

Super did stick around. He, too, seemed to be convinced that he was responsible for being at my side as I carried and delivered his pups. Daily I would sit on my nice pile of crushed leaves or abandoned wool from a devoured sheep. Super would bring me the most delicious meals from dumpsters behind major supermarkets and refined restaurants in Hightown. This life would be better than any other time in my life. Better than when I was with my mama and brothers, and definitely better than when I lived with the Gregg's.

At night, we would cuddle and snooze together. He would lay his front leg over my body as though he was afraid some other wolf would come by and dognap me. As time passed, I did get fatter and bigger. I was sure some puppies were cuddling inside me. One day I felt a slight quickening where I assumed they were hiding out. I yelped and called Super to my perch under the willow.

"I felt a quickening. I'm sure your puppies are beginning to move around inside me. Before you know it, we'll become proud parents of little wolfdogs that look just like you."

"And you, my dear," my sweet wolf mate added.

"Do you think it's time that we move to a more secluded spot?" I asked Super. "You can't always be near me, especially when you're out hunting or dumpster diving. Do you know of a cave or old shed in some out-of-the-way location where we could birth these puppies?"

"Why don't we scout around this afternoon? You look like you could stand a little exercise after just gestating these few weeks. You need to get up and move so you'll be fit and have the energy to push my puppies out when the time comes. Maybe the next full moon?"

He was right. I was flabbier than I'd ever been. I was almost embarrassed. I looked like a fat mutt when instead I should have a regal look about me. Time to trim up so I would make Super proud when the time for motherhood came.

"It's a nice day. Let's go now, Super." I was standing up and doing some stretches as I waited for his answer.

"No better time than now, my love," he said.

We decided to walk farther down the road, to search for some old, abandoned shacks out in the middle of a field or perhaps an old spring-house along a creek that no one used anymore. To be truthful, the little birthing center I was hoping to see didn't seem to exist. Every building we set our eyes on was in tiptop shape, which meant the owners were still using it, or in such sad shape, it looked like a soft breeze would crush it. No place for *my* pups.

"We're getting quite far out," I finally said after what seemed like all day. "Let's go the other way. Maybe on the edge of town, we'll find something we can raise our puppies in, where you can get to the dumpsters more than once a day."

Super thought that was a good idea, so we set off toward Hightown. Just outside the city limits, there it was, the home of our dreams. It looked like an old garage. A fire-devastated house was nearby, which meant that probably no one lived anywhere on the grounds. The door was unlocked. We walked in. This time of year, it was hot inside. That made me think that when the puppies came, the warmth would still be lingering for them.

We jumped on an old, discarded mattress like two puppies ourselves. I could envision myself laying on it in a few weeks and starting to introduce my tits to my puppies. Lots of room to spread out and for the pups to run around.

"What do you think, Super? Is this a good place to squat for a few months, at least until the puppies can get out in the fresh air and learn how to hunt for themselves?"

"I like this," Super said. "Let's stay here tonight and see what happens. Maybe that mattress is already spoken for by a homeless person. If so, we'll have to move on or scare him away for good."

So, Super took off for another dumpster dive while I moseyed around in the garage to try to spruce it up a little, making it into a restful nesting place for our new little family.

Darkness set in, and Super was still not home. *Odd,* I thought, but I wasn't too concerned. Maybe there were slim pickings tonight or Super was stocking up so he could spend more time with me in our new little garage apartment.

The moon tonight was a slight sliver—a crescent moon, some would call it. I began to worry about my dear Super. I knew he had good senses to see in the dark and to also use his nose to pick up the trail to our new place. After waiting what seemed like hours, I drifted off to sleep, expecting to feel his wet tongue on my nose at any time.

Then, I heard a noise that scared me. It sounded like a two-legged creature was coming toward the mattress I was lying on. My senses perked up, and I made a dash through one of the broken-out windows that had an old table below it. I don't even think the creature had a chance to see me because I was so quick and graceful.

So, there I was alone in the pitch dark. The wind had picked up. The moon had disappeared, and I felt some rain drops on my head. There was nowhere to go, and I was frightened. I couldn't believe that Super had not returned yet. I would have to stop being the pampered little bitch and get some sense about me. I took off up the road to try to find the willow tree where we'd settled earlier; our little love nest, so to speak.

I was on the trail of its scent when the storm became violent. Lightning and thunder had replaced the serene moon. I tucked my tail between my legs and started to run through a ditch on the left side of the road. I came to the culvert where Super and I had spent our first night, just after meeting each other. I cautiously entered it as a batch of mice seemed to run out the other end. It was damp there. Water was beginning to run through it. My shivering body seemed to be soaking up the water. This would not work tonight. I crawled back out and continued running down the ditch. There in front of me was a driveway that led to some humans' dwelling. I didn't want to run up to it, because I knew I would have to contend with those controlling creatures, and that was something I wasn't ready for. Yet there were no other choices as the storm was raging even worse and the rain was almost blinding.

I headed to the dwelling's front porch. Maybe I could stay there until dawn or until the storm subsided, and the people who lived there would never know I had even taken shelter there. But it was no use. A dog inside started barking.

I wanted to bark back, like all good dogs do, to tell it to shut its mouth. But it insisted, like all good guard dogs do, on protecting the humans who fed it. I jumped off the front porch and ran to the back of the building where a door was cracked open. I nestled into the opening and was just going to sleep when I felt a dripping tongue on my soaked ear. I had been found, and this time the dog was practically body-to-body. The smell was familiar. Too familiar. Then I knew. I opened one eye and saw Racer standing over me.

"Well, who do we have here?" the dog whispered. "I know I told you that you could come here sometime, but I didn't expect you so soon."

"Shh," I whispered back. "Let's talk in the morning. I've been running all night. I'm so worn out."

"Well, you might as well come in and lie on some dry floor until it stops raining. C'mon," he urged.

Shivering and scared, I walked inside Racer's owners' home. I wanted to stay as close to the door as I could, so I could make a mad dash out when the rain subsided. But Racer would have nothing to do with that. He motioned me to lie on a rug by the kitchen stove where roasted meat odors surrounded me.

Since I hadn't eaten for many hours, I couldn't get to sleep while saliva was dripping out of my mouth, and my nose wouldn't stop smelling these delicious odors.

"Hey, Racer, Racer, RACER," I yelped. "I'm so hungry. Can you give me just a few nibbles of that meat I'm smelling? I have puppies in me that won't stop jumping around."

By now, Racer had run into the Winters' bedroom and was begging Mrs. Winter to come out into the kitchen. I heard her tell Racer to shut up and go to sleep. But he persisted. To shut him up, she got up, and after a few steps, she saw me curled up on the kitchen floor.

"Floyd, Floyd, there's another dog in the house! I told you to check that back door before you came to bed. Well, now here we are with another dog. Get out here and shoo her away. I bet she's got puppies, too. Damn bitches. Always breeding more puppies to overrun this area. Floyd, get out here this minute."

In came the zombie of a creature I assumed was Floyd. He was a heavyset old man in his underwear, with a big round belly that looked like it could hold three litters of pups.

"Aw, she's kind of a pretty puppy herself." He squinted his eyes to see me better. "I like that funny spot over her eye. Give her something to eat, and she'll be fine. And come back to bed. We'll decide what to do with her tomorrow. Racer's a good watch dog, isn't he?"

Chapter 20

All I could think after I was fed and left alone in the kitchen after everyone else, including Racer, had gone back to bed was that I was relieved to be safe and satisfied.

But my sleep became troubled. I was a wild dog in a house dog's house. I'd promised myself that I would never be dependent on humans again. Meanwhile the storm raged on, and there was no way I was about to go out in it, even if my scruples insisted otherwise.

I methodically circled a pillow the Winters had put out for me. Racer came into the kitchen and told me to calm down or I would be put back out in the storm. I couldn't win, it seemed. This was the stud who'd sweettalked me to get what he wanted, and now I was nothing to him but a ragged stray.

And I couldn't stop thinking of my beloved Super, who, as far as I knew, was still out in this vicious storm. Perhaps he was looking for me and worrying that I was dead. Thus, the rest of the night went by slowly. I promised myself that as soon as daylight came, I would run away from this house, rain or not.

I saw lightning flash in the sky. The rain was still coming down, however. I closed my eyes, and I was out of it until Mrs. Winter kicked me away from the stove. Stunned, I rushed away and curled up by the door. I yelped to be let out, pretending that I had to relieve myself.

But Mrs. Winters was preoccupied with getting breakfast on the table. I saw Floyd come out in the kitchen, so I yelped and barked this time. All I heard in response was, "Shut up, you bitch."

So, I peed right there in front of the door. And for that, I got my nose rubbed in the puddle. No human had ever insulted me that way before. I sneezed and sassed Floyd. Then, I scratched on the door and left marks proving I had done so.

Racer strutted over beside me and told me to cool it. I was getting nowhere with the Winters acting like a spoiled pup.

"I am not a pup," I insisted. "For all you know, I could be carrying your pups right now. Can't you see how much fuller I am now than when you left me in a lurch?"

"Could care less, bitch. We both had some fun that day. But that day's long past. You're beggin' for your safety now. So, get humble."

"Can you let me out? I've got business to attend to. I have no time to linger around the likes of you and your human family. Look at what I just did. They wouldn't let me out, and I had to go. Other stuff is coming out soon if you don't open this door and let me shit."

"Why you looking at me, bitch? I can't open a door, especially with it being locked. Just hold it in. Would hate to see 'em rub your nose in shit."

So, I stood there by the door with my sad little face. Don't get me wrong. I'm a proud canine. No way do I enjoy buttering up humans, but a dog's gotta do what she's gotta do.

Floyd spoke up, "Well, let me go out and see what damage the storm did last night. Seems it rained its guts out, hon."

"Well, don't be long. Breakfast is about ready. Would hate to see it get cold on you. You know how you get when you have to eat cold food."

"I'll be just a few minutes, hon. And can you wipe up this mess your dog made? I already rubbed her nose in it. You get to clean it up."

Mrs. Winter frowned but took an old rag and wiped the pee around the door up. "If you want to stay here, little lady, you gotta shape up and do your business outside. Now, I can see you're with puppies, but that's no excuse."

She threw the rag in the garbage, washed her hands, and flipped the eggs without breaking the yokes. It had been a long time since I had smelled frying bacon and eggs early in the morning. Saliva started to drip from my jaw.

"Want some?" Mrs. Winter asked. I walked away over to the door again. I wouldn't give her the satisfaction of thinking I needed her kindness. But before I knew it, there was a slice of bacon on a piece of old newspaper right beside me. I picked it up with my long tongue and barely chewed it before I swallowed it. I looked back at her, trying not to beg. But to be truthful, I did beg for another piece. And I got it. I kinda thought she liked me.

But Floyd was something else. I sensed a mean streak in that man. He had said I was kind of cute last night, but other than that, I think he'd rather I got lost than mess up his routine and his ruling of the house.

As they sat down to eat, with Racer begging for crumbs at the couple's sides, Floyd brought up the subject of me. "Shall I put her out now and let her go on her way, or shall we keep her and see what her litter's like? We could make a little money off of her if we play our cards right."

This I didn't want to hear. My mind went back to that old woman who had separated me and my brothers from Mama and sold us. I still missed Mama. And no litter of mine would be taken away from me. Once more I went to the door and yelped to be let out. Both humans ignored me like they'd chosen the second option. Would I become a prisoner in this house until my litter was born? And what would happen to Super? He would think I'd deserted him, that I didn't really care for him at all. Or maybe he was hurt somewhere and was calling out for help. I looked around the house for an opening, such as a window, where I could jump out and go look for my partner. No such luck, it seemed.

Mrs. Winter found one of Racer's old collars and tightened it around my neck and behind my front paws. From now on, if I was allowed outside at all, it would be on a short leash, Mrs. Winter told me. And some days when neither of the humans had time to walk me, they tied me up to the clothesline instead. I could bark and yelp all day. They would yell for me to shut up but wouldn't let me loose. I couldn't wait for the day when my puppies would arrive. Maybe then a way would open up where all of us could escape.

Days at first went slowly, but eventually they turned into weeks. I looked up in the direction of the moon on nights when there were no clouds. I could see it getting fuller. For some reason—probably because Super had said so—I figured when the moon became full, a miracle would happen. I would deliver my pups.

I didn't know much about birthing back then, or how I would know when the time came. I definitely was getting bigger, but not as big as I thought I would get. I worried that my puppies weren't normal, that they needed me to be more settled in my predicament. So, I forced myself to be just a little friendly with the Winters and even Racer. They would never have guessed that it was only an act. Meanwhile, Racer was let out every morning and was allowed to gallivant all over the land-scape, probably looking for more bitches to mount.

Every day, I looked forward to being tied up on the clothesline. At least I would be outside where I could watch the bugs, rabbits, and other wildlife run and scamper with freedom. Summer was beginning to bear down on us all. By now, the puppies inside me were outgrowing their space. I ran back and forth along the line, hoping to get things moving so I could at last see my puppies. That night, the moon greeted me with all its fullness.

My full womb, almost like clockwork, began to harden. No pain. I would lick my tummy area when pain began. But no way would I let the humans know that anything different was going on with me. I didn't finish my dog food that night. I just stayed on my pillow and pretended to be asleep. Sometime after all had gone to bed, I delivered a big puppy that I wanted to hold up like a trophy and bark, "Look what I've done! A strong male that one day will lead the pack."

I had hardly calmed myself down before I felt another tightening around my middle and the urge to push. This time, the pup came out easier. Another male, but this one was skinny, gray, and long-legged. I knew immediately that the strong pup was Super's, and the lean runt was Racer's. Nevertheless, my maternal love sparked, and I caressed both. I licked the afterbirth off of them. (Really, it tasted somewhat good.)

I did my best to get the pups to suck on my tits, which now were alive, warm, and delicious from new hormones circulating in my body. "Hey, little ones, c'mon. Take a taste. You won't break me. My body has nourished you for the last two months. It wants to nourish you now with my milk. C'mon, baby boys. Grow strong. Grow to be wild and free."

Chapter 21

I had stepped into another milestone of my life. A few months ago, mating with both Racer and Super had brought me sublime happiness and fulfillment. And now being able to bring life into the world emboldened me to know that I was part of the Creator's means of keeping life going for us dogs—and yes, even wolves.

I named the boys Leader and Follower. I envisioned Leader one day being the alpha for a large pack of wolves. Follower would make a good pet for a family with lots of children. This all kinda sounds like I had higher hopes for Leader than for Follower. And maybe it was true.

The next morning, Mr. and Mrs. Winter found me with my puppies. "Well, isn't this sweet," said Mrs. Winter. "Two darling, healthy-looking pups. And one looks like our Racer, if I do say so myself."

At the sound of his name, Racer came over to look for himself. "Not bad, little Blackeye," the dog whispered. "Looks just like his dad. But this other one? Not me at all. Doesn't even look like you. You were getting around, weren't you?"

Okay, so dogs can mate with more than one dog. That's part of their freedom as free dogs. Ironically, the one I had the biggest hopes for was the one Racer and Mrs. Winter didn't seem too impressed with.

Then walked in Floyd. He picked up both puppies as I looked on with pride. He put the gray skinny one, Follower, back to my breast. But he kept Leader in his hand. My gaze of pride turned to fear and anger as he stuffed my wolfdog puppy in a plastic bread bag and took the puppy outside with him. I rushed to the door to go with him, wherever he was taking my pup, but he kicked me back into the house, and Mrs. Winter locked the door. I stared out the door's window. It was there that I saw Mr. Winter drown my perfect pup in a gallon plastic bucket full of dirty water.

I jumped high enough to reach the handle of the door, but I couldn't unlock it. I yelped and barked, growled and cried as the old man stomped on my pup in the pail, crushing his fragile bones and squeezing all the air from his lungs. I didn't care about the runt left on the pillow. My favorite offspring had just been violently killed by a human, and there would be no justice.

Chapter 22

Just a few hours earlier, I had experienced a highlight of my life. Alone I had birthed two healthy pups from two fathers. The pups had latched on to my ample breasts. I had gloried in being a new mother.

Now, all of my joy had been stomped and killed like Super's son out there in the pail. Even though I was still recovering from my delivery, my love and mothering hormones went crazy. I slammed into the locked screen door and broke through in an effort to save my first-born pup. I used my nose to tip the pail of bloody water out and clasped my teeth around my dead pup, still beautiful in my eyes.

I no longer had any interest in my other runt pup. It would be left to the Winter family to raise him, by feeding Follower baby spoons of cow's milk from now on. I was out of here with my dead, beloved pup. In order to respect him to my fullest, I would carry him in my mouth to my favorite willow. And there I would devour him so his flesh would live on in me.

As I ran away from this evil place, as fast as I could considering my post-delivery condition, I stopped often to look at what I had left behind. Yes, I was leaving my offspring to those mean people and Racer. How could I, as a mother, do this? This abandoned pup represented all of what I hated in my small world. At that particular moment, I had no maternal instinct to nourish Racer's offspring. Later, I would find out that these extreme feelings of love and hate were normal for first-litter mothers. We would often not realize that what we delivered was new life. Thus, we would either eat our pups or ignore them altogether. And here I was doing both.

Once I found my willow tree, with its leaves still shedding the rain drops from another rain, I circled around my favorite place and settled down on the wet earth. I was at last hidden from the cruel world that didn't understand me, one that didn't really care about me and considered me trash.

I washed my dead baby wolfdog, still warm from lying close to my caring body and sucking my warm milk into his tiny tummy. He looked so much like his daddy. He would have grown up to do what his name said: lead a pack of wolves. To be honest, I wasn't sure other full-blooded wolves would have accepted him as the breeder of the pack. But if he was shunned by the pack, he would have organized his own from other wolfdogs and canines.

Ever so gently, I forced open Leader's eyes. I wanted to see if he would have the light-colored rusty pupils that red wolves had, or if he had dark eyes like my own. Although I couldn't be sure, I saw in him the eyes of his father, which warmed my heart while also leading me further into depression.

I put him to my breast. All of the tits were filling with milk, waiting to be sucked into newborn pups. Now, they would be confused. Where were the baby pups they were made to feed? I hoped beyond hope that somehow there was a small spark of life left in this baby pup at my breast. Maybe the smell of my milk would revive him. I even prayed to the dog god to be merciful and bring life back to my firstborn, to bring the life now in Follower and transfer it to Leader. The dog god could sacrifice Follower for Leader. But that was not to be.

So, after I'd cleaned him as gently as my mama would wash me, after I had checked his eyes and loved on him, I commenced to eat him, morsel after small morsel. He was delicious. I felt as though his soul was being reborn within me, and that someday, that mighty soul would be reborn as a pup who would develop into a wolfdog, leading a pack into healthy old age.

Many humans may wonder how I could devour my own child. To me, such an act demonstrates the ultimate closeness of one dog to another, that rather than let other creatures of the wild eat my baby, I did it to show my great love for every organ, bone, muscle, and fragment of this body that was made from me and returned to me.

After the meal of my son, I washed myself. I had forgotten how pushing Leader from my body had torn me in the birth process. Leader was huge for a newborn pup, and I was still small, still growing myself into a mature bitch. As I pampered my tired, bloody body, as I tasted my own blood that had caked around my behind, I wondered if I would ever be able to have any more puppies away from the cruel judgments of humans. I needed my partner, Super.

Somewhat clean after my big ordeal, I was finally able to drift off to sleep. Maybe by sleeping I would discover that all that had just happened hadn't really happened at all. I would awake still with my puppies inside me. Don't all females have at least one bad dream before they give birth? Well, I'd had mine. Things would be back to normal when I awoke.

Chapter 23

Yes, I finally woke up, but prematurely. My stomach was rebelling from my newborn pup being digested. Throwing up woke me up. And I was riveted back into real life, probably the most horrible part of life that I had ever experienced, hoping I would never be put through sorrow like this again.

I moved slightly away from the vomit and tried to go back to sleep. But the smell of the vomit was so stinky that sleep wouldn't come. Rather than leave my special spot, I forced myself to again eat my pup's remains. This time, he slid down my throat easier, like he wanted to be back in my tummy. He was honored, and I was honored, that he had been a part of me so many times. Perhaps his spirit would protect me in the months ahead. He would give me the strength of wolves. I would be a member of his species rather than a puny little dog known for a dark spot over one eye.

I began to moan because of the pain in my body and especially in my heart. I needed Super there with me. He would be mad. I was sure of that. And I would be mad because he had deserted me when I'd needed him the most. Why hadn't he come to look for me? Or maybe he couldn't. Maybe he, too, was dead. And that would make me alone in the world.

But when the world seemed its worst, a fascinating creature dropped into my life. It was in the willow above me, trying to climb beyond its trunk. The creature was making too much noise up there. Surely, it knew that willows weren't made for climbing. Its branches, if you wanted to call them that, were like twigs that arched almost to the ground.

Then, the creature fell out of the tree, expelled by one of those twigs. It landed on all fours. It had a yellow coat and smaller ears than a dog's, but its whole body was smaller than a dog's. At first, I thought it was another canine species, until I remembered back to my day at the vet's office when similar animals were hissing at me.

I took a chance and tried to talk to this creature. I doubted that we would be able to communicate at all. But what the hell. I said, "Hello."

To my surprise, it answered, "Who do you think you are, sitting here under my tree?"

"Your tree? I'll let you know that I chose this tree months ago, lots of memories ago. Never saw you around here."

The weird animal responded, "That's because the Humane Society had me then. Ever heard of it? Kinda like a jail."

Shivers went up my spine. "You mean they have jails for animals? Do they kill you there?"

"Some of us get killed. And some of your kind do, too. That's if you don't get rescued."

"Oh, another project from humans," I said. "What kind of a dog are you, by the way?"

"Do I look like a dog, one of your kind, to you? I haven't seen myself in a mirror for a few weeks, but I'm certainly not one of your disgusting breeds. People around these parts call me and my species cats. You know, like you are a dog, we are cats. I can't believe you've not run across our species here and there. Humans absolutely love us."

"You gotta be kidding. I thought they only loved dogs like me. I've been trying to get away from them my whole life, and they always seem to find me. What are you doing out in the wild right now? The only time I've seen creatures like you was at the vet's, but most of them hissed at me."

The cat laughed. "Yeah, we like to scare you dogs. It works all the time. You dogs are such pushovers. Like you call under a willow tree being out in the wild. You're out in the middle of a pasture where about the only other wildlife you'll see are a few mice, opossums, or skunks. And you don't want to see the skunks. If you do, that means you're too close, and they'll spray you. Takes weeks to get their smell off you."

Just like the cat said, as it edged closer to me, I got nervous. I realized that it was smaller than me, but somehow it also seemed smarter, like a trickster.

"My name's Old Pat. What's yours?"

"Blackeye," I answered. I think the cat was trying to get me to relax.

"Blackeye? You gotta be kidding me. Why in the world would you give yourself such a crummy name?"

"Well, I don't know if Old Pat would win any prizes for originality," I shot back.

"It used to be Old Tom, but there were too many of us, so I changed it to Old Pat. Are you male or female?"

I was insulted. "Look at me. Don't you see my tits? I just delivered pups last night. I'm recovering."

"So, where are the pups?" Old Pat asked.

Tears blinded me and I took a big gulp. "That's a long story. I deserted one and ate the other."

"Aw, must have been your first litter. Yeah, mama cats when they have their first batch sometimes do the same thing. You'll do better next time."

"I hope there is no next time," I said between howls.

"You'll get over it, sweetie. As though you can't see, I'm a tom. I get around and have mated with maybe hundreds of females. How come they never got you fixed? Was it because of your funny-looking eye?"

"No, I ran away. I never want to be tame. But I was due to be fixed any day at the time. Now, I kinda wonder if maybe I should have just gotten fixed."

"Don't let 'em do that to you, little lady. Yeah, sure, life out here can be rough, but nothing beats freedom, not even those tiny cans of cat food or cat movies, you know. One thing I've noticed, however, is that we cats—we know how to put humans in their place. You dogs are a mess. Always panting and wanting to play with the humans. No— humans love us, but they know that we need our privacy to meditate and sleep, especially sleep in a nice warm window."

"So, you're a male, and I'm a female. You'll not bother me, will you, like want to mount me or smell all my private parts?"

"Little woman, I am not even the least little bit interested in your sexuality. Has no one ever told you that cats and dogs don't mate? Sometimes we even hate each other. If you were a real dog right now, you'd chase me up that tree."

If I'd felt better, I would've. But my birthing pain seems to be crippling my whole body, especially where I'd torn to push Leader out. "Give me a few days, and I'll show you how much of a dog I am. Tell me, are you a wild cat?"

"Am I a wild cat, as opposed to what? Is there any other way to be a real cat like my ancestors, the lion, the tiger, the cougar, even the bobcat? I may not impose the fear factor that those felines can, but in my heart, I'm a tough ol' tom."

"Well, you can go on your way now. At least you took my mind off my loss for a few minutes. I've got to sleep and gain my strength back. So, just go on now."

Old Pat looked at me, and I swear I saw a small bit of compassion in his eyes.

"Aw, shucks. I'm not too busy right now. I'll stay here and watch over you for a while. Let me bring you some water and something to calm your stomach. You need some tender loving care right now."

I was amazed at Old Pat's offer of kindness, especially since he was another one of those males. Perhaps male cats and female dogs could get along. Maybe even be friends. I didn't know I was about to enter the world of interspecies relationships.

Chapter 24

As I took another nap and tried to digest all my sorrows, Old Pat was there. But when I woke up, he was gone. Seemed he'd given up on me too.

My eyes filled with tears. I howled and mourned the loss of my babies. I knew one was still alive, but I had no maternal instinct to nurture that little guy. I was sure the Winters would give him the care he needed.

In the middle of my lonely pity party, Old Pat showed up dragging a small container of water and a chicken leg.

"Here you are, little lady! Let's get your strength back now. I stayed here with you until you started to stir some. I put myself in your place and thought you might need some water and food. Here, help yourself."

I had never run into a creature quite like Old Pat. He was the only one who had treated me special with no strings attached. I wondered if that was because I had never talked to a cat before.

"Are all cats as nice as you?" I asked as I lapped up the cold, clear water. "Why are you being so good to me, a stranger? Is it because I can't chase you up a tree yet?"

"No, I really don't know why I'm being nice. I'm usually an old grouch. But we wild animals, we need to stick together. We're dying out, don't you see? Every human now wants to own one of us and make us their baby. They even have strollers for us now and clothes they squeeze us into. Nope, I stay away from those kinds of people. Then, there are all these groups that claim they want to save us from the mean old world out there. They trick us with mouth-watering treats, then put a bowl over our heads. Before we know it, we're in a truck to the Humane Society, where they put us in a cell. We gotta do our business in a small litter box, and if we don't get fixed and adopted—well, then we're *humanely* killed with a shot."

"How do you know all about this? No one ever told me about what humans do to keep us out of the wilds. I already have gotten shots, but I didn't die. Not yet anyway. Does it take a few months, or what?"

"Aw, you probably got some of those vaccines humans make. 'Sposed to keep you from getting sick. My opinion is we get sick because we're around all those germs humans carry on them. They live in denial. Plain old human smell ain't good enough for them. They shower off their natural protective layers about every day with fancy-smelling soap that, if it gets in your eyes, hurts like thorns from a berry bush. Then, as if that weren't enough, they put on what they call deodorant and aftershave, or perfume or cologne in places where their true smells come out. For some reason, they don't want to smell like their own species. No, they want to smell like flowers or trees."

"Golly, how did a cat learn so much?"

Old Pat took a nibble off the chicken leg. "Well, comes with age," he said as he chewed. "Have the older dogs not discussed this with you ever? Maybe we are smarter. Tell you what. We cats are suspicious. You dogs want to be friends, lick the enemies' faces, snuggle with them. You play ball with 'em. You roll over and beg for 'em."

"Know what you mean. Like even going to tea parties with 'em and being dragged all around on leashes." Now, I was talking and chewing at the same time.

"Yep, we're not too crazy 'bout leashes. I don't know why you dogs are such wimps. You got no pride in who you are?"

We both took a minute or two to lick our lips before gulping more water. I pondered Old Pat's question before taking my next bite of my chicken wing.

"Hmm. Never thought 'bout that. I know I wasn't happy being treated like what they thought dogs wanted. I always thought I was different from other dogs, who seemed happy being the playthings for little girls and boys, and even their big people."

"To tell you the truth, Blackeye," Old Pat said, lifting his front paw to his chin, "I think those humans have a self-esteem problem. They get with us and think they can make us love them if they give us canned food, if they groom us and give us a seat to sun ourselves on the windowsill. Don't they know we're just manipulating them? Never saw a dog with any brains love their master the way books and TV claim they do. Of course, humans know we cats ain't crazy 'bout them, because we will scratch and bite if we feel like it, or if they touch us where we don't want to be touched. Like right here behind this ear. Drives me nuts."

For a moment, I forgot my pain and started pondering the knowledge Old Pat was sharing. I labeled him as the Guru Cat. He was finally explaining so much that I hadn't been able to figure out for myself yet. Of course, I was still young. I'd probably find out on my own someday. Certainly cats, who were smaller than us and who had less room in their heads for brains, weren't as smart as us dogs. But Old Pat sure came close. Had to admit that.

"Want to gnaw on this chicken bone?" I asked him.

"What, you want to give me a chicken bone? Here I educate you and bring you food and drink, and you want to kill me with a chicken bone? Don't you know that's one of the fastest ways you can kill us cats?"

"Nope, didn't know that. Maybe I shouldn't eat 'em either?"

"Probably not a good idea. Those chicken bones, they get real sharp once they get torn apart, and when you swallow 'em, they can mess up your digestive tract in a bad way. You know, chickens and most of those flying creatures, they're dumber than both of us."

"But they know how to fly. We don't. And I've heard mockingbirds mimicking other birds. And you say we're smarter?"

"That's what I said, little lady. You can believe me or not. Up to you."

Chapter 25

From that day on, Old Pat taught me so much about cats and dogs, domestic and wild. He also cued me in on how crazy humans were. How they worried about the tiniest things, like what color of sheets they laid on (even colors we'd never seen or heard of), and how they loved fruits and vegetables (also never seen or heard of). How they would usually bear only two children, and then for nearly 20 years they would spoil them, sending them to school most of the time and to summer camp when school was out. The more I found out about humans, the more I wanted to avoid them forever.

Since Old Pat and I were different species, I didn't have to put on airs around him, and he certainly didn't around me. He would make me sick because he was constantly licking his fur. Sometimes he would throw up this icky stuff called hairballs. I told him that was because he was obsessive-compulsive about licking his hair, but he paid me no account. That cat sure did teach me lots of big words, however. I bet you can see that already.

Like Super, however, he loved dumpster diving. We especially liked these fancy restaurants' dumpsters where we could find almost a whole plate of Chicken a la King or smoked mussels. I had to admit that humans had mastered the art of cooking meat and eggs. I left the asparagus and fruit salad alone, though.

One particular night, just as the sun was touching the western mountain tops, we stopped at the McDonald's on the way back to our willow tree. We looked both ways before we jumped into the dumpster, whose lid had been left open by the last employee to dump uneaten food in it.

As Old Pat and I were arguing about whether McDonald's chicken or hamburger was better, another employee, probably just getting off work, slammed the lid back down on us while we were still distracted. As much as we tried to squeeze through every little peep hole, we were stuck. Stuck all night, by the way. And what made things worse were the rats and mice that revealed themselves after we had finally given up on any possibility of escape.

Old Pat thought maybe we could reason with them. They would stay on one side of the dumpster, and we on the other side. Nope, they wanted to nibble on us while they also gorged themselves on everything we'd already avoided. I don't know how they could eat so darn much of everything. They were like vacuum cleaners. Pooped as fast as they ate. Both Old Pat and I tried to refrain from breathing, the smell was so horrible. And their little claws were like pins running up and down our bodies.

They had no manners whatsoever. I never wanted to kill any animal as much as I wanted to kill those varmints. But Old Pat warned me against that, saying they were full of diseases that could kill us. These, being dumpster critters, were bad. Out in the wide-open spaces, yes, it was okay to eat a mouse or a rat occasionally as part of Old Pat's Code of Ethics and Good Health. But to eat those in dumpsters, that was asking for trouble.

After a night in which we seemed to be caught in hell, morning brought us a ray of hope. The varmints had eaten their fill. We were absolute messes ourselves. A teenage human came by. I guess he wanted to dumpster dive his breakfast before school. He was shocked when he saw us, surrounded by Happy Meal boxes, staring up at him.

He slammed the dumpster lid shut. We could hear him on his little phone thing. I shivered thinking about whom he could be talking to.

Maybe his mom or a buddy? I know it wasn't his cat or dog. Old Pat and I huddled together in the corner of the dumpster. The teen's head kept peering in as he cracked open the dumpster's lid. I could tell he thought he was saving our lives, but I prayed he'd just turn around and go off to school.

Then, a van drove up. A couple of humans got out, carrying poles with mesh stuff at the ends like they were going to go butterfly hunting or fishing. But they were there to capture us.

"Oh, oh," Old Pat groaned. "It's them. The Humane people. They're going to take us to animal jail. Our only way out will be by getting rescued or accepting death."

"What the hell?" I barked. "We can't end our lives like this. Maybe they want the rats and mice, not us. We don't need rescuing."

But only Old Pat knew what I was saying. I figured our time in these beautiful mountains and their big dumpsters (minus rats and mice) was coming to an end. No chances would come my way to be a mama dog to hungry puppies in months to come. Old Pat seemed to look old and even scared. This time, we'd blown our chances for a *happy ever after* story. Or so we thought.

Chapter 26

Neither Old Pat nor I were dead yet. We'd been dumped into a box truck with a bunch of other cats and dogs. One of the noisiest places I'd ever been. Hardly any of us knew what was up or in store for us today.

Old Pat was stoic. "You just as well settle down and endure the ride," he told me. "You're cute and still young. They won't kill you unless you growl too much and bite everyone that comes near you."

That's what I wanted to do. My life with Old Pat had been going well, with the exception of last night in that nuthouse some call a dumpster. But we assumed all would be well the next morning when someone would open the lid, and we would jump out. Damn that young boy who thought he was rescuing us dumb animals.

The road to the county animal shelter was a bumpy one, which only added to the chaos we animals felt inside the truck. Most of us were either barking or meowing. A few cowered in the corners of the truck and hissed or moaned during the entire trip.

The truck stopped, finally, and the driver put it into reverse. Then, *thump*. The truck's rear hit what seemed to be a solid wall. The gate at the back of the box truck rolled up, making a scary noise. There, smiling and pretty humans greeted us with soft tones and outstretched arms. I knew their strategy. They didn't want us to react violently against them, so they acted like we were welcomed guests. Okay, if they wanted to play their way, I would play my way. I wasn't ready for the shot that would put me to sleep forever, so I melted into the embrace of the woman who brought me to her shoulder.

"Welcome to the Animal Shelter," she said as she lovingly smiled at me. "What's your name, sweetie?" As if I would bark it out to her. She was a short human with protruding beige teeth. She was covered with a paper robe and wore rubber gloves. I could tell she was nervous. A person never knew what one of us wild animals would do to someone who thought animals were gifts from the Creator to be transformed into adoring pets.

She put a plain collar on me with some stick figures on a tag attached to it. She put me on one of those silver tables like the vet had done and took a deeper look at me. "You need a bath," she announced. "Once we get you through with that, we'll give you a nutritious meal and let you nap for a bit while we process you."

Uh oh. Isn't that what they do to pig meat when they make it into sausages? Were they going to process me so soon? I wiggled in her arms and tried to escape. Another worker, maybe her boss, grabbed me more assertively. In turn I bared my teeth, letting both know that I wasn't there for a casual visit.

"Show me the exit," I howled. Of course, neither of the handlers understood me. I think they thought I was just scared—in shock, or something like that.

"A young female," the boss lady said. "Looks well nourished. But she really needs a bath." She yelled at the driver, "Where did you find this little cutie?"

"In a dumpster over at McDonald's on Mountain View," he yelled back. "She was with an old tom. Looked like they'd been trapped in there overnight."

"You did right gettin' them out of there," the boss said. "We'll give her antibiotics so she doesn't come down with something."

Meanwhile, I was still baring my teeth and growling at as many of the workers as I could. I was also looking for Old Pat. Seems we got separated. I was put with other dogs in this section of the building. Old Pat was probably over with the cats. I already missed his wise companionship.

"She doesn't seem to have been neutered," the boss lady noted. "Write that down, Melody. We'll have to get her fixed before we adopt her out. With that black mark over her eye, they'll all want her."

This boss lady was a tough human. She caught me off guard, spread my mouth open, and peered inside. "She's got all her teeth. By the looks of 'em, I would say she's not much more than a year old, but certainly old enough to be fixed. I think her tits show that she's already had a litter or two."

With those words, my heart felt like it would pump itself out of my chest. I didn't want to be "tamed" or "domesticated" by these women or any of the humans who would be coming here to "rescue" me. If any human "adopted" me, I would run away. But even before that happened, I promised myself that I wouldn't allow them to "fix" me. I didn't know how, but somehow, I would defend my fertility and my right to give birth if I wanted.

After I was checked in, so to speak, Melody slowly dipped me into a tub of warm water. Hate to admit it, but I couldn't help but relax as she "sudsed" me up, being careful to keep the soap out of my eyes. Afterwards, she wrapped me in a fluffy brown towel before shoving me into one of their cells, where there was a bowl of dry dog food waiting for me.

"Now, you relax and eat your fill, little girl," Melody coaxed. "I'll be back soon to take you outside where you can romp and relieve yourself."

Then I was alone in the crowd. On every side of me were other dogs, from mere puppies to mean old Dobermans. They weren't any happier than me. We all wanted to escape. Oh, there were a few exceptions. I guess they were the ones who had given up on life itself. They had tried to be friendly to the humans. They were polite and ate the food that was given to them. They seldom barked. But they slept a lot. Maybe they knew that any day now their days would come to an end.

Even among all these dogs, the animal I missed most was Old Pat. I was worried about my pal. Thoughts about what might lie in store for the two of us troubled me constantly. When I closed my eyes after the sleepless night in the dumpster, I would see Old Pat looking deeply into my eyes and telling me that all would be well.

"Just play along with 'em," he would advise. "But keep your eyes open unceasingly. Look for an escape. Some worker will be distracted, and you'll get your chance. I'm doing the same where they put me. There's a pond down the road from here. It's surrounded by lots of brambles. Head there, and when the other of us escapes, we'll meet there. Got me?"

I assured Old Pat that I understood. I kept envisioning our escape and meet-up; the sooner the better.

Melody came by as she had promised, about mid-afternoon. She attached a leash to my collar and dragged me outside where there were other dogs smelling one another, growling, trying to hump, and eating other dogs' poop. Some were just bathing themselves in the sun, dreading the moment they would have to go back into their cells and listen to all of the other unhappy dogs, including themselves.

I looked for my escape route. At first, the fence around us looked pretty tough. But the ground was soft. I imagined myself hurriedly digging my way out, maybe over there by that bush. I'd never planned something like this. But then I remembered how I'd escaped from the Winters' home by sheer force. I would have to get mad and make a dash once again.

As we walked back into the shelter, I noticed the cat area. There was Old Pat curled up in his cell. It looked like he'd had a bath, too. His bowl of dry cat food was still full. I knew that Old Pat had trouble with his teeth. He never ate hard stuff. My heart was breaking as I saw my friend lying there like he'd given up.

"Don't give up, pal," I shouted in a bark as I passed the row of cells he was in.

The following days became a blur of activities. A vet looked at me and gave me a shot of antibiotics. She prescribed some stuff for my fur, which had become coarse and dry. They debated shortening my tail, which I emphatically argued against. Of course, they didn't understand my barks. Very few humans can do that, but they did get the message, due to my loud outburst as the subject was discussed. Melody gave me a dog manicure and pedicure, which also bugged me, almost like she was invading my private spaces.

And then came the big subject. When would I be spayed?

"Since she's currently not in heat, I would like to schedule her for as soon as possible," the vet said. "You know the surgery takes longer when their female parts and blood veins are engorged. I would say this is a good time."

"Help, help!" I howled to Old Pat. I knew he heard me. But he didn't respond. What could he have done anyway? Today, tonight, early tomorrow morning, or right before they prepped me for surgery, I would escape. If necessary, I would risk my life to be free.

They set the time for fixing me, which meant removing everything inside me that made reproduction possible. I would never be able to have puppies again. According to these smart people at the shelter, there were already too many dogs in the world without loving human homes. And after the surgery, I would be much happier, so happy that I would probably get fat and lazy.

I didn't want to be cut open, to have parts of who I was removed, to be sewed up and be itchy as I healed. I didn't want to be put to sleep and be completely vulnerable to a human who really didn't understand a dog's way of looking at life.

All night long, I gnawed on the wires of my cage. I tried to scratch a hole in the bottom of it. I tried to dislodge the latched handle. Nothing worked. At about dawn, I gave up and decided my only option was to take off when the handler opened my cage. I knew if I was mad enough, worked up to a frenzy, I could be Super Dog. I was in perfect condition, the vet had said. And I felt perfect. Now, it was just a matter of time.

The other dogs started to stir. Some were barking and howling. Some were still snoring. I told the neighbor dog that I was going to make a run for it. Did she want to go with me? She passed the word down the line. We would all go at once. Create mass confusion for the staff. Some of us would make it. Others wouldn't.

And Old Pat? I was sure he would find his way. I would hang out over by the pond for a few days, hide out near the shelter and watch for signs of his escape. If need be, I would be with him after his possible death sentence. I shivered to think of that.

I wanted to tell him to perk up and get adopted by some old woman who needed an old cat. Then, he could escape and save his life. But I never got a chance to tell him. He was smart. Surely, Old Pat had already thought of this himself.

Chapter 27

The alarm clock at the receptionist's desk started our day. That was when the staff got to work, and we dogs were taken from our cells to do our business outside. I looked at my neighbor, a dachshund, and she gave a look at the mixed breed next to her, and the same thing happened all down our row and moved on up the next line across from us. Staff, leashes in hand and ready to click onto dogs' collars, were opening up the cages.

But this morning would be different. First, I revved up and squeezed out of my cage on the right side of Melody. I would have never imagined getting through such a tight opening. Once my hips were out behind me, I was gone. I took a quick look at my fellow dogs. Most of them were getting out fast too. We were all barking, and the shelter was in a perfect state of chaos. At this point, we were all on our own. I decided to head toward the front door.

Wrong decision. It was still locked. I thought quick on my feet. Where could I go? Maybe the big door where deliveries were received? I dashed over there. A sliver of light shone on the floor, meaning the door hadn't been closed all the way. With my nose and some creative paws, I squeezed my tough body out just in the nick of time. A hand had grabbed my back right leg. I had no time to think about my next move. I bit the hand that had fed me. I know it was not a kind thing to do. But I didn't have rabies, if that meant anything in my defense.

So, at last, there I was out in the parking lot. Dogs were running all over the place like bees swarming out of their threatened hive. No time to socialize. My destination was down the road until I came to the pond, where I would shelter in place until Old Pat came along.

Aw, freedom! I could taste it, smell it, run with it. No more cages for me, ever. I'd die first.

Off to my right, I saw a grove of what looked like blackberry bushes, a stand of brambles. I was almost there. I heard a vehicle come up quickly behind me. I didn't dare turn around and look. I had to keep going. My instincts told me to seek a hiding place, somewhere that was too tight for humans to get into or through.

As I ran along and got beyond the thorny bushes, a barbed wire fence became the obstacle challenging me. I noticed a place where I could possibly squeeze myself under the fence. I had to take a chance. Even if I got cut into slices, I would crawl into that field and run like hell even beyond the pond, until the animal catcher was a distant memory.

The grass in the field was tall. Good. Getting under that barbed wire scraped my skin and left me with a bloody coat. Not so good. Nevertheless, the animal catcher was still at the fence trying to figure out a way to get over it. I was afraid he might have wire cutters or shoot a tranquilizer arrow at me. If he opened the fence with wire cutters, goats grazing in this field would get out, and it would be his fault. If he hit me with the tranquilizer, and it hit a vital organ, I would be dead, and that too would have also been his fault. Old Pat told me all about them. I wanted to yell at the animal catcher to give up and just let me go. I wasn't worth the effort.

I knew I had to stop somewhere soon. I still hadn't pooped or peed yet, and I was so thirsty. I told myself that once I got to the back side of the pond, I'd take a drink and leave a dump as a souvenir. While I was making my plans, my pursuer was still trying to come up with a scheme for how he would get to me. He was getting farther behind me. He needed to just give up.

Recharged, I continued my run. By now, it was little more than a trot. My eyes were always looking for a good place to hide out. A big old tree came into view. If only I were a cat and could climb up it. But second best, I saw a big hole in the tree's trunk. There were still leaves from last fall inside it. I jumped in and busied myself forcing the leaves on top of me. Not a perfect spot, but I had to take a chance. Even if caught, I promised myself I would run away again, even if I had to mangle my captor's entire body.

I stayed in the old tree's hollow for what seemed hours, or until the hills on the horizon started to melt the sun above them. Surely, it was safe to come out by now. My nose was first to emerge from the leaves inside the tree. Then, I poked my front paws out, with the top of my head and eyes darting up, down, and across, giving me the *all-clear* confirmation. All was relatively quiet. I then got up the nerve to expose my whole self. All I heard were crickets and locusts scrubbing the day off their wings. I smelled no humans. No news is good news, some say.

By now, I was so hungry that I salivated at the thought of eating the mice and rats in the dumpster from a few nights ago. I decided to lie perfectly quiet in the tall grass. Some little creature would come along, something I could swallow whole, so I wouldn't have to crush it to death with my teeth.

Maybe if I remained in the wild all my life, I would grow to assert my toughness, to kill unapologetically, to take my place on the food chain as a predator.

So, tonight, I took a step in that direction. I became a sleuth. And sure enough, a small vole poked its head up out of a hole. I snapped off his head and started to chew, bones and all. So much for previous intentions. I was so hungry that I enjoyed being a predator. As I closed my eyes to sleep that night, I thanked the little vole.

A couple days passed. I had by now moved over to the pond to wait for Old Pat to show up. I decided to give him one more day. He didn't come. Fears for my own life were now replaced by fears for Old

Pat. Why wasn't he here yet? He was smart enough to escape. If I could make it, he could. Plus, as a cat, he had numerous opportunities to climb up higher than people could reach. All I could remember was Old Pat curled up in his cage with a defeated look on his face, and an untouched bowl of cat food. Was he resigned to a fate that I wouldn't even let myself consider? I had to think of my dinner, I told myself. This was too depressing.

The day finally came when I could no longer stand my isolation. I would take a chance, go back to the animal shelter, and see what I could find out about Old Pat. The full moon was guiding me as I snuck back in the middle of the night. All was still. I moved in closer to the edge of the building. Surely there was a security guard around here somewhere. I couldn't be too careful.

My ears perked up. I heard lonely moans within the walls. There were a few loud and fierce barks. Did they know that they would be killed if they exhibited too many behavioral problems? Between the barks I heard a few mournful meowings. I thought I could pick out Old Pat's meow if I heard it. I didn't. But he may have been asleep. Who could know?

I checked the gate from which I'd escaped a few days ago. This time it was locked tightly. Then, I looked at all the doors around the building until I ran into an old man smoking a cigarette under a light pole.

"Get out of here, you old bitch. They're filled up right now. Come back tomorrow and see if they have a vacancy," he joked.

I scampered away with my tail tucked between my legs. *Lassie* came to mind. Besides *Lady and the Tramp*, Sara sat me down to watch old *Lassie* episodes with her on that screen of talking and moving people. Lassie would pester people to save lives just by barking a lot and wagging her tail until they followed her to the place where people were in danger. I got up the nerve to do my Lassie routine on the guard. I had no other choice.

I got up close to the old man, barked over and over, wagged my tail till it hurt.

He blinked his eyes and opened them wide, wondering what could be bothering me so much. Was there a fire starting somewhere in the building? He smelled his cigarette, perhaps wondering if it was marijuana instead of tobacco.

"Shut up, dog!"

I looked into his eyes, now wide-awake. Then, I turned my face quickly at the shelter he was guarding. I trotted ahead a few steps, looked back at him, begging the guard to follow me.

He stood up. I think some kind of hormones in him were giving him energy to get into this *Lassie* episode. I started to move faster, turning to look at him every few steps to urge him on. The guard's heart seemed to be softening. He was actually enjoying this adventure as we rushed to the shelter together.

At the shelter's door, he whispered, "Okay, bitch, we'll go in, and you can show me what's going on. But stop the barking. We gotta be quiet as butterflies. When you see a camera, duck. Better to just crouch the whole time. If anyone finds out that I let you in, I could lose my job. Understand?"

If the occasion hadn't been so crucial, I would have yelped in laughter at his sign language. I tried to assure the man by nodding my head and closing my mouth. I was on a roll. I couldn't believe this old man. He trusted me. He would have made a good Jeff from *Lassie*.

"Remember, quiet. Now, show me the problem." He motioned as he unlocked the door. His next move was to disable the alarm system as I dashed out of sight to the cat area and started to look for Old Pat. He wasn't where I had thought he would be. I took another long look from one cat to the other. Not one even resembled Old Pat.

I decided that I was too late. He was probably in that big freezer now waiting to be shipped to a school where Old Pat told me kids learned how to cut open dead animals. Carefully, I commenced to crawl back out, when I suddenly saw the yellow trademarks of my friend.

"Over here, buddy," the familiar voice whispered. "Psst, psst. I'm over here near the exam room."

I looked in that direction, and there was Old Pat. Skinnier than I'd ever remembered him, but alive, nonetheless. I snuck over to his new cage and with little trouble moved the handle to let him out. Our luck; it wasn't locked. Maybe the shelter folks didn't think he was important enough to lock him up. No problem. I wouldn't have locked the cage either.

We gave each other a lick and a smell to be sure we were legit. Then, we crawled out as quickly and quietly as we could. The guard was at the wide-open door. We marched through it, and the place was locked up one more time. No one seemed to notice, except the guard, who must have been let down that there was no big fire or monster roaming around inside the shelter. Nevertheless, as we started our journey back to the pond hideout, I turned and did a big bow toward the guard. He nodded, seemed to smile, and lit another cigarette.

"Let's get back to your hideout," Old Pat suggested. "We can catch up when we both feel safe again. I want to get as far away from this place as I can. I missed you, buddy."

Chapter 28

We walked the rest of the way to the pond, where we felt safe. The night was warm and the moon bright. The only noises were the familiar sounds of the frogs looking for some fun in the calm, protective pond.

"Sorry, I don't have any particular spot for you to settle into tonight. I should have thought ahead," I said to my friend, breathless and much thinner now a few weeks after our capture. While Old Pat had been gone and I'd lived in fear, I'd learned to feed myself from the pasture around me and the pond just feet away.

"I still haven't adapted to preferring raw wild food," I admitted to Old Pat as he lay on his spine and spread his legs out in every direction.

"Aw, but this life and this place make me feel so good," he said, as though food needn't even be mentioned at this time. "Sure, I might nibble on a young rabbit about now. Food from a can would make me vomit. But forget food for now. It will come when we're ready for it. At least we're out of that jail down the road, and we don't have to consume those lumpy hard nuggets probably made from rendered animals. And by now, you would have been fixed. You'd be a zombie dog just wanting to eat, sleep, get petted, and be led around on a leash. Me? Tomorrow, I was going to be euthanized–killed. You came just in time, buddy."

"I know, I know," I nodded. "I'm a spoiled house dog wanting to have gourmet food out in the wild. But to tell you the truth, it's not been an easy road for me either. I've been lonely after losing my first puppy litter. I've been scared shitless, hungry, soaked. I'm not even two yet, and I've had my share of downs. Very few ups. Am I barking up the wrong tree here, Old Pat? Maybe dogs need humans after all. But when we move in with 'em, they want to control us. There is no middle ground, it seems."

Old Pat nodded. "Why, I've lived with both humans where I've been pampered with the most expensive gourmet food, been combed daily, allowed to sleep all day if I wanted, and put up with complete boredom. No, wildlife with its downs is still better than the ups with humans." He had a big yawn. His eyes told me he wanted to sleep.

"Okay, I know you're exhausted, old man. It's been so long since I had anyone to communicate with. We'll talk tomorrow. I'll try to find a fish in the pond over there for your breakfast."

"You spoil me, little lady. Yeah, we'll talk and talk and then hunt and hunt tomorrow. Good night." Then, he was asleep.

I moved over to the hollow in the tree, which by now was beginning to smell like me. It made me feel welcome, like the old tree and I were now part of one another. I was the salve covering the hurt in the old tree, and the tree gave me protection, I reasoned.

The frogs sang me to sleep with their rhythmic chanting. My pal was back, and the future looked bright. Would Old Pat and I go back to dumpster diving or perhaps just go through neighborhood garbage containers? Would Old Pat teach me to finally appreciate fresh food from all that lived around me? Could I get used to being a predator? Would I fall in love again? What did Follower look like now? And whatever happened to Super? Was Sara okay?

Chapter 29

Those damn birds woke me up just as the dark blue of night was turning into a pale gray with a tinge of peach reflected from the pond. I tried to return to my sleep wonderings, but I recalled I had company. Hadn't I promised Old Pat I'd catch him a fish this morning?

Ready to get myself all wet during the early morning chill, I forced myself to climb out of the tree hollow and get to work. I passed by Old Pat, still in the same position he was in last night. What an adorable old critter he was!

After many splashes and misses in the pond, I was finally able to clamp into a small bluegill. I could see the silent frogs looking on. I was sure they would make fun of me after I left. One day, I'd get even by making a meal out of a couple of them, I told myself.

Triumphantly, I presented the still wiggling fish to Old Pat.

"Hey, Pat, wake up," I yelped. "C'mon, old pal. We got a big day today. We're both free as the bees." I put my paw on his shoulder. He didn't respond. I was getting worried. I put my ear to his mouth and smelled him. He didn't seem right. Dead? Like Mrs. Gregg, who died holding me?

I admonished myself for even thinking such a thing. He was just worn out. I would be, too, if I had endured life in Old Pat's cage as long as he had, where dogs were always barking and cats always hissing and meowing and scattering litter into other cats' cages.

But for now, I would wait. The fish stopped wiggling. It was finally dead due to lack of oxygen filtering through its gills. But Old Pat also wasn't wiggling or moving in any way. There was a fly on his nose, and the old feline didn't seem to care.

The sun was bright by now, almost halfway on its way to directly cover me. I had to wake him up. "Okay, buddy. No more snoozing. Upsie daisy!"

He didn't respond. I tried to roll him over, but he was stiff. I remember back to when Rolf died. The way Old Pat was not responding was like when we pups finally realized that Rolf wasn't one of us anymore. And now Old Pat wasn't with me anymore either. Like far too many times in my life, I was alone again, deserted. On my own.

I didn't know if I could take all of this one more time. You may have never seen a dog cry, but I did cry that day. All day and night. I threw the fish back in the water, where he floated to the other side. I'd killed him for no reason. I certainly had no appetite to eat anything.

It was like another chapter of my life had ended. I had nothing to look forward to. I even considered going back to the shelter, letting the vet operate on me and take all those parts out of me that made me female. Someone would adopt me because I had this beautiful black patch on my short white coat. I was truly a beauty, but I didn't feel that way at the moment.

There were also the Greggs. I knew little Sara would be overjoyed to see me scratching on her front door. Within a few days, Mr. Gregg would take me to the vet so I could be fixed. I wasn't ready for that. At *least not yet*, I surprised myself by thinking. Before I had said never. Now, it was only *not yet*.

I crawled into my hole in the tree then. I decided it was okay to be sad, to mourn. I didn't have to move on today. I didn't have to eat or play or hope or bathe. I just had to be. And maybe figure out what I should do next.

I had a hard time getting comfortable in the old tree. Was she also disappointed in me? Did she want me to move on and stop bothering her? But finally, we came to an agreement. I would be allowed to stay for a limited amount of days, and then I needed to move on and discover more of this huge, foreboding world.

Chapter 30

I couldn't stop crying. My mouth became salty as my tears dripped into my mouth. I took my paws and tried to wipe them toward my neck. How could a dog cry just because an old cat died? But attachments aren't always dependent on what species animals belong to.

What good did it do to rescue Old Pat last night, to risk my life for him just before he was to be put to death with a needle this morning? Why hadn't I tried to save him sooner? Why did I wait so long? Was I a coward at heart?

Then, I told myself that at least Old Pat had died free in the wild, the place he loved to be. Yes, I was late, but together we got out. That old guard learned something about animals last night. Our intellect and spunk led us out of that place and near this peaceful pond, even if it was for one night only.

There were no more tears to cry out. I discovered that I hadn't done everything wrong. Best of all, winning over all the negatives was this fact: Old Pat died a happy cat. And I helped him get to that special place where he could pass in peace.

I was still depressed, mostly because I was alone again. Old Pat was supposed to teach me some new tricks to help me live with wisdom in the wild.

"But you have me, my friend."

Who said that? I wondered. I knew it wasn't my imagination. And who was *me*? It sure didn't sound like Old Pat. Was it his angelic voice, with more of a feminine quality?

"You know me," the voice teased me. "I'm Jennifer Gregg, Mrs. Gregg, Sara's mama."

"Oh, you. Gotcha." I half believed, half didn't believe, that the voice was real.

"I've been on your trail for months now, Blackeye," the voice continued. "I haven't spoken to you lately because I was enthralled by your energy, your zest for living in the wild. Even when you lost your beloved Leader, I marveled at your courage and how you honored Leader's body and blood by eating him. And not just once, but twice. And then there was Old Pat. What a wonderful and respectful friendship. You're my hero, Blackeye."

I thought I must be dreaming. Was Mrs. Gregg still around? I opened my eyes and saw the same misty, woman-shaped cloud right outside the tree hollow. I wanted her to hug me, but I knew she couldn't do that. We could only transport our sometimes vocal, quiet utterances and thoughts to one another. Nevertheless, I was completely confused by this special moment, another example of different species interacting, like Old Pat and me.

"So, what do I do now, Mrs. Gregg? I'm lost. I have no friends out here in the wild. I'm tired of trying to fit in. I'm banging my head on a brick wall, and I'm hurting."

"Look at this tree, who has given her body as a home for you," Mrs. Gregg reminded me. "How about the fish that gave its life for you, the frogs who serenaded you last night? The gratitude Old Pat felt for you when you came and rescued him last night? And—"

"Okay, I get you. But all that is mostly in the past, other than this dear old tree here," I complained.

Mrs. Gregg wouldn't give up on me. "Let me tell you, my sweet lady. You are still young and beautiful. You're leading a life of freedom that so many other canines would love to have the courage to do. You have that courage, and it will become easier. Trust me."

I couldn't argue with Mrs. Gregg anymore. She was smarter than me—deader than me, too. Did she know what the future would bring so I wouldn't have to discover it on my own?

"I will depart now, my child. Remember, you can call on me any time. You are my link with the real world. But your link with freedom mesmerizes me."

Then, she disappeared. But she left behind a new sense of purpose in my life. Things still weren't perfect. But there was a spirit on my side. Too bad she had once been human. I would try to overlook that for now.

Chapter 31

Jennifer Gregg put a spirit of vigor in me. She was gone now, but her words were in my heart. Maybe there was a chance that my life could change, that everything I loved wouldn't be taken from me. I was still young. In the name of Mrs. Gregg, once a human, I would again try to carve out a place for myself in the wild. I would do more than walk on the wild side. I would run into it. I would dance where my ancestors only survived.

After I dug a burial hole for my friend Old Pat and pulled his body to it, I reluctantly laid him in the cool, welcoming dirt. I covered him. Before I stomped the dirt down hard over him, I considered digging him up and taking a couple bites from his flesh, just to show him that I wanted him to be part of me forever. But then I thought of his beautiful body, his perfect yellow coat. He wasn't my puppy like Leader had been. He was my friend. I decided to let him enter his cat kingdom intact where he could always be proud.

I would be lying if I said I skipped away from my friend. Nope, I dragged my feet away. I turned around multiple times, either to be sure there were no varmints trying to dig him up, or to see if he would jump out of his grave and run to catch up. But when I reached the road, I took one last look and let my best friend go.

I didn't know where I would go, but I knew I would get as far from the animal shelter as possible. When I saw the van that had caught me, I made a right turn, leading up to the Blue Ridge Mountains.

Staff were leaving work when Melody saw me. She pointed me out to the other workers, and I ran like hell. I think Melody knew me well enough to know that I wasn't cut out to be a rescue or even a fostered pet. Besides, it was quitting time. They had to get home to prepare their meals and feed their kids. So, they changed the subject to dinner menus and let me go.

Fall was drawing near. The trees were pouring themselves into a costume change to celebrate the many shades of the dying season. Within an hour, I was climbing a mountain. Humans gave names to the mountains, but we dogs didn't pay attention to such names. All I knew was that I was on some kind of trail, hoping it belonged to deer and not humans.

Keeping my eyes peeled for a hideout in which to spend the night, I slowed down, my breath becoming labored as my altitude got higher.

Then, I noticed the smell of the forest reviving me. I hadn't sensed these smells for months. I became nostalgic for my younger days when I took off for my vision quest. It was funny. The senses remembered the smells, the sounds, the sights, but I had a hard time remembering the insights that had been handed to me at that time. As I got deeper into this new environment, many of my learnings would come back.

It certainly looked like good surroundings for a cave where a lonely wild dog could find safety and sleep. And how I needed that tonight.

Twilight turned into deepening darkness, and still I had found nowhere to lay my head and body. I couldn't go any farther. I left the trail, curled up in some weeds, and I was gone from the world. I slept so hard that I didn't even dream. Was I going to become a hibernating animal like the bears and the squirrels?

I woke up early the next morning when I felt a nose on mine. It was wet and slimy. Whatever it was didn't make a sound. I shook and opened my eyes like someone had set off a firecracker inches from me. Our eyes met. I saw a fox looking me over. Relieved that the fox wasn't a bear, I postured myself as the bigger, smarter animal and higher up on the food chain than the fox.

Even though I'd been able to communicate with Old Pat, I figured cats were smarter than foxes. I'd never heard that foxes were sly. Thus, the fox spoke first.

"You're kind of out of your habitat, aren't you? You a dog? I've heard some dogs get tired of the humans caring for them. You one of that kind?"

I shook my head. I was still drowsy and wanted to be left alone. Maybe the fox would understand. "Can you go away?" I asked as politely as I could, not wanting to anger this curious creature.

"You ever hear the saying, *the early bird gets the worm?* Well, it's also true for every other creature up here, two-legged, four-legged, flying, or crawling. This is the hunting hour. You hungry?"

"Not really. Check back later." I closed my eyes again and tucked my head under my two front paws.

"Don't say I didn't warn you, you spoiled, domesticated—"

With that insult, I was up on all fours. "Those are fighting words," I barked. "I asked you to leave. Now, leave."

"Aw, get a life, little doggie. You'll be okay once you get moving. I can show you where the fish are, baby rabbits, a few squirrels, if you're hungry. You might say I'm the happy hostess of these woods. I welcome you newbies and chase away those we don't want 'round here, if you know what I mean."

"Hmm, prejudiced, huh?"

"Some residents here might disagree with that, but you're kinda right. We gotta be careful in these dense woods. It's a live and let live community. I don't bother or eat you if you don't bother or eat me."

I was getting grouchy about now. "So quit bothering me then," I barked. "I walked a long way yesterday. I ache and am in mourning. I need time alone. Get lost."

"Okay, okay. I gave you a chance to be a part of this neighborhood. Now, you'll have all of us out to get your tail."

"Yep, sure, you're right. I'll deal with that when it happens. Now, good day."

By some miracle, I was able to fall back to sleep. When the sun was directly over me, another nose rubbed against mine. At first, I thought the fox had come back to bother me or chase me out of his neighborhood altogether. Coming to my senses, I realized this was no fox bothering me. This was something much bigger and more threatening. The bear, whose presence I'd always dreaded, was nudging me. I'd always feared something like this would happen. With black bears all over these mountains, I shouldn't have been surprised.

I needed to act tough. "Okay, you guys win. Just let me leave now," I yelped as I uncurled myself and stood up, reaching the height of the bear's shoulders.

"I would say so!" the bear growled.

"Nice knowing y'all. Know any other neighborhoods where they're looking for new residents to move in? I'm not much trouble, other than perhaps going into heat about every six months to a year. And come to think of it, that could be about any day now."

"I wouldn't send you to any of the neighborhoods here in the Smokies. Why don't you be a good doggie and move in with a dogless couple down by the river? You'll get free meals there, and they'll get you fixed so you're not plagued with *seasons* all the time. Sometimes, I kinda wish that someone would fix me. I'm tired of cubs following me around everywhere. Now, git!"

I ran down the mountain, wondering the entire way why Mrs. Gregg had steered me wrong. Of course, she hadn't told me to ascend that particular mountain. Maybe I had misunderstood her. But for now, I had to find another home regardless of what she really meant.

I wondered and wondered as I wandered and wandered. Dogs don't read maps. Really, dogs don't read anything. I'm lucky that I can talk, but most dogs don't do that either.

I wanted to go back home. Not to the pond, not to the Greggs' home or the Winters'. I didn't want to cross paths again with Racer. No, I wanted to see Super. I wanted to go into the woods where I had learned about myself, not far from my old stomping grounds. I remembered the smells of the area and a few landmarks. Maybe if I heard a certain car on the road or a rooster crow, I would find my real home where I could live among the wild animals for the rest of my life.

For now, I would have to use instinct to find the right way home. Surely this world wasn't that big. I must have been from one end to the other by now. So, I continued to walk and look, to listen and smell.

Along the way, I found a few fish in creeks, and those ever-present mice. "Did anything taste familiar?" I asked myself. Then, I would answer, "Don't all mice taste the same, wiggle when they get in my throat, and give me the hiccups and awful burps afterwards?"

It seemed days, maybe even a moon, before things began to come together. There was that old smokestack by many tanks and big, box-like, ugly buildings with lots of windows. The smoke had the acrid smell I had noticed when I lived with the old woman after she stole us pups from Mama. Then, there were the chickens—all sizes and shades, speckled, and a few roosters here and there. At last, I could sense I was close to where I had met Super. I spun around to look at this part of my world. I saw the culvert, where I'd gotten all wet in the storm. And off far away, but really closer if I could actually see it, I saw the woods where I'd first found myself and my purpose in life.

Fear built up in me as I remembered the Winters' and how angry they probably still were with me. Of course, I was mad at Floyd more, since he'd killed my favorite son. If they saw me, if Racer saw me, what would happen?

Perhaps I would play dead. Could I stiffen up like a dead animal, not make a noise if something tickled me? What if Sara caught a glimpse of me? Now, I remembered why I didn't want to come back here in the first place. I might get caught. But then, I might see Super again.

I would move forward after dark when most humans were inside, afraid to go out in the dark, chilly night. I would roll in the mud, hoping it would cover up my familiar scent and color.

Most humans—and hopefully all the animals—wouldn't recognize me after I completed my camouflages. Still, I stayed in the ditch for as much of the way to the forest as I could. I tiptoed (or tip-pawed) as long as I could, knowing this was slowing me down too much. But now I could almost taste the forest. I passed the old willow, now losing its leaves for the winter. Then, a few breaths later, I was there. I was home again.

My senses went into full force. My smeller rejoiced. My hearing whistled. My taste buds wanted to eat anything put in my mouth, and my eyes popped open with tears glistening in the moonlight. Now... *where, oh where, was my lover?*

I could feel my body doing and feeling strange things. I spun around knowing that soon I would be charged with life-giving and mate-seeking hormones. I knew who I wanted. I hoped he knew and wanted me, too.

Chapter 32

Sometimes, I think that humans claim to be the only creatures who can love in such a way that is unselfish, going as far as sacrificing their own lives for the lives of others. I say this to let you know that we—the other mammals and even reptiles, birds, bugs, and plants like trees and flowers—we all love. Love is a commonality we all share if we exchange oxygen and carbon dioxide. There was a time when I didn't know this, but I learned it along the way of my life in the wild. If we didn't have love raging through our veins, could nature be as diverse and coordinated as we find when we walk through the woods?

Yes, this was the woods of my spiritual awakening—another level that animals can reach, not just humans. I was back where the leaves of the trees were more yellow, the soil richer, the smells more fragrant, and the sounds more harmonious. I'd never been to heaven, but I imagined it must be like this place where my hormones were beginning to rage and where I was becoming giddy.

I sat down in the tall grass that had once been my bedding and licked my rear. The smell and taste of fertility was exhilarating. In a few days or maybe a week, I would be in full heat. My thoughts went back to my first season, when I had been so naive. This time I would be aware and more assertive in choosing the father of my litter.

The previous months following the birthing of my first litter had been so tumultuous. I wanted peace this time before and after birth.

I would need help. I knew that. While many of my sister bitches seem to just go through the motions of survival, I was looking for a partner who would marvel with me the miracle of new life beginning, growing, birthing, and maturing within our lives.

More than ever, I knew that I had to nourish myself, exercise, and sleep. So, first, where would I go to pursue my food? I had to consume protein, and that would be mostly meat from other animals now running through these woods. It was about time to accept that I was a predator. I would never enjoy killing. I hoped that within a few days I could at least tolerate it.

The most delicate brownish rabbit ran toward me. I hadn't moved in minutes. The poor little feller probably didn't identify me as a danger to him. As it hopped straight toward me, I started to salivate. I wanted to eat this creature. I bared my teeth. I hardly had to get up on all fours. Before I knew it, I had bit into its jugular vein. As far as I could tell, the rabbit felt no pain. It had been alive one second and dead the next. Its body went limp in my mouth.

I thanked my fellow creature for giving itself to me, and then I went about eating it. I savored the freshness of its flesh, the tenderness of its muscles, and the richness of its internal organs. I endured the fur, spitting it out bit by bit. I left the bigger bones to lick and gnaw on before I would drift off to sleep.

I was satisfied. There was no guilt. Was I at last becoming a true part of the wild culture? Was I forgetting the morals of human civilization and integrating the code of the wild?

Did I want to sleep here in this tall grass all night? Or should I scout around for a more protected area? So far in my travels, I had not been successful at making a home for myself. This time that trend had to turn around.

After licking my paws and around my mouth, tidying myself up to an acceptable level, I got up and looked for a good spot to relieve myself. Many of us animals choose and mark our own places for pooping and peeing. I found mine without much trouble, a place other animals, according to my nose, had ignored. This would be my spot, by the pile of sticks. I didn't know why there was a pile of sticks. Surely, they hadn't organized themselves. I didn't care. I just had to go.

When I returned to my spot where the rabbit bones were, I circled the spot I wanted to lie in and then crashed. Tomorrow would be my day for wandering. I would find a real home and maybe take a bath in the creek.

Chapter 33

During the night, I was serenaded by a hoot owl. I breathed with the hoots and was lulled into one of the best nights of sleep I'd ever experienced.

But all good snoozes must come to an end. If they don't, then we're dead. So, the birds let me know that, indeed, I was still alive. By now, some of the bird population had left these woods, knowing that food would be sparse in the months ahead. Yet the remaining flying creatures made up for their absence by singing louder and longer.

"Okay, okay. You can now let up now," I barked. "I'm up. Where's my breakfast?"

They were quiet. Maybe no other creature had ever tried to communicate with them before. I guessed it was up to me to manage my own meals from now on. Today, I would search for a fish or two.

On my way to the creek, I noticed that I was leaving behind a stronger fertile scent. I turned my head back to my tail. I was getting soft back there and tender to the touch. My tongue took a quick swipe and tasted a tinge of blood. Things were moving along fine. My body was preparing. And so was I. I would take an invigorating bath. A clean body was necessary for a healthy litter, I told myself.

I smelled activity over by the creek. A couple deer were there with their fawns. A buck was on the watch. Beavers were leaving their dam work in order to rest up for the day so they'd have the energy to continue their work tonight. I turned away and hid behind a tree when I spotted a black bear with two cubs taking their fill of fish for breakfast. They needed to eat gluttonously since they were preparing for hibernation within the next few weeks.

I kept my eyes on all these animals and their fish for a long time. I was about ready to leave and come back later when I noticed the bear and her cubs scampering off into the cove.

At last, it was my turn. I tested the water. A little on the cold side. No soapy lukewarm bath for me like I'd had at the shelter. No, this was like cold water from ice cubes. And there was no soap. For that I was glad.

I forced myself to completely submerge my body so I would get over the fear of being cold. I had to toughen this body so it would be prepared for the activities ahead. And if I thought it was bad now, wait until mid-winter. Maybe my litter would come in the dark of the winter like I had.

The sun began to reach over the treetops and aim its rays on me. I experienced something like a warm hug on my back as it arched above the water. Then, there were the fish. Which would I pick today? A trout; a slow, old catfish rummaging around below my feet; maybe that turtle over there; or the silent frogs hoping they were blending in with the weeds around the creek banks?

Before I could decide, I noticed over by the turtles a familiar-looking guy with rusty brown eyes. A big dog, maybe a wolf. It couldn't be him, could it? Had he picked up on my scent so soon?

I pretended to ignore him. I showed off instead, performing my doggie paddle, floating on my back. He started to eat the fluttering fish he had just caught so effortlessly.

I traipsed out of the creek, soaking wet, and sulked over to this supercharged male and shook off every drop of water that still clung to my coat. I glanced over at Super. Handsome as ever. His rich brown coat with black and white highlights gleamed.

He looked at me and winked. "Want to share a bass?"

At this moment when I should have been sublimely happy that my Super was alive and not dead, my anger began to simmer, and I growled instead.

"Why did you desert me that night? How dare you go off and leave me in that shack? I waited and waited for you. But you never came back. A man came into that shack and scared me half to death. I was out in that storm. You remember that storm that night, don't you? Weren't you worried about me at all? You deserted me when I needed you most."

Super let the bass slip from his mouth. I couldn't tell if he was going to explain what had happened, or if he had indeed died and came back to life.

"So, I see you're mad at me. I've been waiting and looking for you all over here. How do you know I didn't come back that night? There was no man in that shack when I came back. But you were gone. Why didn't you wait for me? I had brought you all kinds of food. It all spoiled. Did you decide you liked Racer better than me?"

Now, I was fuming. "Don't you dare mention that piece of rat poop to me. I was stranded in that storm. I was sure I would die. I found a front porch to hide under. He found me. I hid by the back door, and he found me there. Finally, I was forced into his house as a prisoner. The Winters could tell I was going to have pups, so I had to stay there until I delivered."

"I would have been there had you told me where you were, Blackeye!"

Now, remembering those unhappy days at the Winters' home, I broke down completely and buried my face in my paws. "Didn't you think to smell around the different farms and houses? I wanted so much to be with you. I had no feelings for Racer, nor did he for me. I had two pups. One was a copy of you, who I named Leader. The other looked like Racer, who I named Follower."

"So, where is my son? I want to see him."

"He's dead."

The silence between us was too loud for my heart.

I looked into Super's eyes, now filled with tears. "Racer's owner drowned him because he was a wolfdog. I abandoned Racer's pup. I don't know if he survived or not. I escaped that day and ate the body of Leader. That was the only way I could show him that I loved him."

Then, we both cried. Super put his foreleg around me. Our sobs turned into slumber. Two lovers together again. So much sorrow between us. It seemed that all the love in the world couldn't relieve the pain we both felt.

I awoke first and eased my way over to the fish and started to lick its natural oils. I bit into the gills and the belly of the bass. *For all his faults, Super was still a good provider*, I told myself.

Super opened his eyes and closed them again when he noticed that I was beginning to stare at him. I didn't know about all the loves he'd had since we'd gone our separate ways. But nature was nature. Would I be able to accept that someday?

Chapter 34

I was still mad at Super for standing me up on that crucial night months ago when I was carrying his pup. But he knew I couldn't stay mad at him. He rested his handsome head on his front paws, waiting my anger out. And considering my erupting fertility hormones that were making me mighty horny, I had to forgive this wolf. I knew in a few days he would be mounting me, and I would enjoy him once more.

When animals are out in the wild, pride has to take second or third place among priorities. Number one priority for us bitches is to find mates who will help us create strong and healthy pups and will grow up to pass on our genes. We don't consciously think this out. We simply are attracted to virile males. The male can be ugly by human standards. Even if he has a yellow and blue coat and tells corny jokes, if he has strong genes, we females are pushovers for his sexual prowess. We don't believe in vets or humans who think they know what's best for us. We want to take care of ourselves and our pups. It all begins with good genes cruising through our veins. And that was why I was drawn to Super. He knew it, too. He also knew that I would build his cubs in my body and nourish his progeny with my rich, nutritious milk. I would be willing to give my life for our cubs.

So, each of us waited for the other to break the ice that was keeping us apart.

I decided to be the one who made the first move. "I'm happy you're still alive and well, Super. Now that my bath is over, I gotta go into the woods and find a place to call home."

"You're movin' back for good?" he asked.

"I'm going to give it a try. These trees and dirt and water are in my blood and bones. I've looked elsewhere, but nowhere beats these wild parts." I edged in closer to his muscular body.

"Let me take you on a walk over that way," he said. "I want to show you something. We can talk as we go." Super looked down toward his paws. "I'm sorry, my lady, that I was missing when you needed me most. Will you forgive me?"

"I don't know, Super. As if you haven't already noticed, I'm coming into season again. This time, not just any lover will get my attention. I might back up to you, or maybe I won't. I'll see how I feel when the time is ripe for mating."

"Good enough for me," Super responded. "But that's all the more reason we need to go on a walk now, way into the heart of these hard-woods. What I'm going to show you will inspire you."

"Let's get started then," I said as I edged closer to him. I didn't want to follow him, and I certainly couldn't lead us. I could tell that he was picking up on my scent. I wondered if he was remembering the happy days we'd had together nearly a year ago.

He wouldn't move. He simply looked at me from my pointed nose to the tip of my snake-like tail. Saliva was dripping from his mouth. "You are some hot mama," he said, while I, now flattered, looked down at my paws.

"Words won't be the basis for how I chose my next mate," I reminded him. "But they won't hurt, either."

So, we walked and walked and walked. I'd never imagined that there were so many ridges, valleys, trees, or bushes on one segment of land as I discovered that day. I now realized that when I'd done my vision quest last year, I'd hardly scratched the surface of this land mass.

"Are you enjoying the sights?" Super asked me as I did my best to keep up with his pace. "This is part of a national forest, so we don't have to worry about humans coming in here to build subdivisions or new towns. We're protected here. Sometimes humans accidentally do the right thing."

"Maybe you're right, Super. But don't tell them that. They can change laws any time they want. They just vote. A leader signs a piece of paper, and we're left without a home. Are we about there yet?"

"There? I'm not going to show you a piece of territory. I'm going to let you see something even more exciting. A tribe, you might say."

"Are there no shortcuts to this tribe? Can they meet us somewhere? My feet ache, and I need to drink some cool water."

Super stopped and smelled me. As he got his nose close to my rear, I became excited, and I could tell he was getting that way, too.

"My, you're a sexy bitch," he growled. "Not time yet, but when you do come into full season, I want to be the one who comes to you, be it in the rain, the wind, or the darkest night. Blackeye, I've missed you so much."

"If you don't get me to a creek or a spring pretty soon, I'll be missed because I'm dead, and we won't get to do anything anywhere," I warned.

We both stopped and heard the gurgling then. I dashed off to the right to lap up as much of the cool liquid as my body could hold. Super had to outrun me, of course. I honestly thought he would drink it all before I got there.

There were tall rocks in front of us, and between the two biggest ones, a steady stream of spring water was seeing the light of day. I stood directly under it, put out my tongue and lapped as much of the silver streak as I could. Then, I did a slight doggie jig, just to show Super how delighted I was to be in his home territory, but especially to have found him again. I could never stay mad at this wolf.

Super looked on and soon was dancing with me. We circled around the stream of liquid filled with minerals. We edged into each other closer and closer, until at last we could get no closer. There we were, two tramps falling in love all over again.

Just outside of our tiny two-dog world, we heard the angry howl of another animal of the wild. "What's that?" I asked, peeved that someone was raining on our mating dance.

"This is what I've wanted to show you," Super answered. "This is my pack. Well, not quite yet. I'm just a former member—one mere wolf like the others. While most of the red wolves long ago died out—you might say were killed—on this side of the state, our small pack has continued. For more than a hundred years, we've successfully survived, hidden away in this territory of caves and springs far from humans. The howl you heard is from our *alpha*, our leader, Almighty. He's old and may soon be cast out from the pack. I want to take his place. There is safety in a pack. We share in the harvest of the hunt. We build strong families."

"I had thought you were a loner," I interjected. "You're telling me now that you don't want to be a couple? What happens to me?"

"I may have to fight for you, Blackeye. Maybe even kill for you. Already the males are picking up on your scent. The strongest will get to mate with you. You and your cubs will become part of the pack, protected by the entire pack."

"But why did you bring me here now? Can't you see that I'm going to be put in the middle of all this? You might get killed and some wolf I know nothing about will have the right to mate with me. I don't want just any wolf. I want you."

"And I want you more than anything in the world, Blackeye. I brought you here today because you have given me the will to lead this pack. I only need to look into your eyes and my muscles tighten, my heart races. I will swim to the ocean, climb the highest mountain, and fight my biggest battle because you will be my prize."

While charmed by his poetic utterings, I didn't like being a prize, like a trophy. I would never belong to anyone, human or animal. "I'm sorry, Super, I won't be around as you fight to be top wolf in your pack. I won't be a trophy to be put on a shelf to get dusty."

"What is a trophy?" Super barked back. "I've never heard of or seen a trophy. How can you say I'm trying to make a trophy of you when I don't even know what such an object is?"

"Oh, you know. In your mind, I might be the biggest bone in the camp, or the best one to sleep with, the prettiest bitch."

It was as if a light went on in Super's head. He nodded. "I guess you then would be my trophy, or the prize for the strongest and bravest wolf. But if you don't want me to do—"

He was interrupted by another howl. We both looked up at the ledge jutting out from the ridge above us. The wolf making all the racket was beautiful himself, virile, reeking of male juices that almost hypnotized me.

Almighty leaped farther than I'd ever seen any creature without wings do and landed in front of me. He gazed deeply into my eyes. He came closer until I started to back away. I thought he might bite off a piece of my flesh. Yet there was something extremely sexy about Almighty. Was he the alpha?

I looked up to the ledge again, where I saw a dozen or more other dogs looking down on us. Were they the eunuchs of the pack? The worker bees? Would I be the queen of the pack? But I wasn't even a wolf. Surely, they wouldn't want to damage the gene pool by introducing a dog into it.

"You are a sensuous and desirable bitch," Almighty said to me. "Why are you hanging with this lone wolf? Come with me, and I will spare his life. If you insist on staying with him, I will destroy him."

I thought now was a good time to introduce a little comedy into the conversation. "My, you're really a handsome fellow, but Super and I... We were just out for a pleasant walk through the woods, and my gosh, you popped up. My name is Blackeye, and his is Super. We'll get out of your way now. Have a beautiful and powerful day."

Then, I really blew it. "Why don't you come over and see us sometime?"

I had hoped this mean old alpha would laugh and go back to his pack. But instead, he seemed turned on by my humor.

"Ah, and this beautiful bitch knows how to make the leader of this pack laugh. Indeed, I think I'm falling in love. I can smell her tantalizing fragrance. Her mark over her eye beguiles me. I will fight for the right to create my Almighty cubs with her. Her little mate here is a lone wolf. He's a loser." The pack howled in agreement. Almighty bared his teeth. He turned around and kicked dust into Super's face.

I had to react, but I didn't know what to say to put a damper on this alpha who had blood on his mind. So, I opened my mouth and let words flow.

"Forget about me. I'm just a dog, and I'm not in season right now. Don't fight over me and hurt yourself. Just let us go on the rest of our walk, and before you know it, this awful scent will be all gone."

My remarks were getting us nowhere. I turned around and saw Super baring his teeth, growling like I'd never heard before. He seemed to have grown three paw-widths since I'd last seen him, about ten breaths ago. Meanwhile I felt that I'd shrunk to the size of a squirrel, motionless by a tree with a walnut in her mouth.

I ran to Super. "Let's get out of here. I know you're tough, but that wolf over there, this Almighty might be tougher and more experienced. You don't really want to get banged up and beaten, do you? You can't mount me if you're all crippled. So, c'mon, let's get out of here."

He heard not a word I said. Not one word. He had his honor and his bitch to fight for. Why had he led me on like this? Now, he had the unbearable urge to fight like he'd warned me. I stepped aside and looked the other way.

I heard bodies slamming into trees. I heard bites cutting through flesh. There were howls to break windows. There were yips and yelps, moans, and cheering wolves all around the battle site. Why did male wolves have to be so mean to each other?

Then, I remembered it was because of little ol' me. Could I settle with being the mate of that wolf now destroying Super? Or was Super destroying himself? I couldn't look. But I do know the fight lasted till almost dark. The sound effects were now decibels lower.

Sometimes, I couldn't hear anything, like they were taking a break. And then there was one long moan. I heard dragging footsteps. I forced myself to turn around and survey the damage. The former alpha was limping away. My Super had whipped his ass and would assume the rank of alpha.

Chapter 35

Suddenly thrown into a new world of wolves, I didn't know how this would affect our love now that we were part of a wolf pack. Since I was a dog, I could be booted out on my behind—or worse, killed by the females in the pack, who also had their own hierarchy. I doubted there would be any chance of instituting a meritocracy in a wolf pack.

But one thing I had going for me was that Super loved me. Would he be persuaded by the pack to mate with the current alpha female? Or as the alpha male, would he bunk the system and insist that I come along with the package? Would I now have to prove myself as the *luna*, or alpha female?

I was tough when it came to fighting for the mate I wanted. However, I was a mere dog, bred for compatibility with humans, not for survival in the wild among wolves. For a year, I'd dreamed of being a true wild animal. Now the opportunity was smack in front of my face. Could I show my stuff? If I somehow was not admitted into this high-ranking level of wildness as a luna, would I still be allowed as a beta or an omega?

Of course, in a wolf pack, only the alpha female would mate and bear cubs for the pack's alpha male. If I settled on being admitted into the lower ranks of females, I would have to kiss future motherhood goodbye. I would have to only gaze at my lover from afar. I would serve as a servant to the luna, if she allowed even that.

Super was near me, licking his multiple wounds. I helped nurse him as he prepared himself to take over the leadership role of the pack. He had to appear strong and of good lineage. For far too long, he'd been an outsider. At last, he'd proven himself by outfighting Almighty, the long-time pack leader.

As I aided him in licking his wounds, some of which he would carry as scars the rest of his life, I questioned him about remaining a part of his life now that he was the leader. Was there any way he could use his influence to bring me in as the luna female?

Although in pain, he managed to laugh, "No way, bitch! You're a dog. The pack will insist that its line not be contaminated by a dog."

"But what if I did battle with the current luna and I outfought her? What then?"

"Blackeye, you wouldn't outfight the pack's alpha female. Often the female is even more ferocious than the male. She would destroy you."

I felt like walking away with my tail between my legs and my head touching the ground. But not before I had my say.

"Look at me, Super. I'm about ready to come into season. If we mate, could you as the alpha male bring me in as the mother of your offspring? If you could have only seen your cub from my first litter! Even Mr. Winter recognized him as a wolf. That's why he drowned him. I can give you an even stronger litter of male and female cubs that will resemble wolves. I'm ready. Mate with me now, so we can enter into this pack as a pair, an assurance that the pack will continue a fine and strong line of descendants."

"Not gonna happen. Sorry, Blackeye."

Now, I was really angry. He was more interested in joining this little tribe of wolves than renewing his love for me. Maybe love doesn't always win after all.

"Then, why did you even bring me here? You acted like you wanted to show me something that would excite me. Instead, you've brought me into a den of wolves. You just fought with everything you had to win the right to mate with me. But now, your pride has taken over your soul." I looked into his eyes surrounded by claw marks—not a handsome sight. But I loved them because I had thought he endured all of his injuries for my love.

"Yes, I fought for your love," Super growled. "I love you more than ever. But I don't think you understand how being an outsider most of my life was hell. Don't you see that this doesn't say anything about my love for you. I'll always love you. But I also love my pack. I've conquered their leader. Now, I must take care of my pack."

I kicked dust into Super's face, where it stuck to his still-bleeding wounds. Then, I howled to the four winds. I was so loud that the birds escaped from the trees. To say I was angry was an understatement.

"So, I guess you want me to get lost and mate with the likes of Racer again."

"No, I can't stand the thought of you and him stuck together. Never!" the new pack leader responded. "Winning over Almighty has made a new wolf out of me, Blackeye. I thought I was fighting to win you. And I was. But now that I have the victory, I have to think first for my pack. I had been ousted years ago, couldn't even be a worker wolf. I wanted you to see what a wolf pack was like, how we had our own society. It didn't quite work out the way I'd thought. Sorry, but I can't give up this opportunity. I could have been killed in this fight."

Then, Super looked at me with pity, like I was a wet and lost kitten.

I have never liked pity. "Look at me, Super. Look. At. Me. I'm better than all these bitches who know nothing else other than what you male alphas tell them. Yes, some of them may be physically stronger than me, but show me one who's smarter. Show me one who's more beautiful. I'm more than a bitch. I'm your lover. You and I are one—have been since we laid eyes on each other. Let me prove that I also can fight. And I will win!"

I may have gone a little over the top with my lecture. But he needed it. All this battling and meanness had gone to his head. Pride was winning over love, or what I'd thought was love. But I had my pride too. And now I understood how its power could overshadow love.

"Let me show you how powerful I am. You know the world is changing. Wolves are endangered and may actually go extinct like the Newfoundland and Texan wolves. We can offer this pack of wolves a chance to enrich its bloodlines by introducing a dog into the pack."

Super didn't seem too impressed with my argument. "Yeah, tell that to the other wolves, and they'll laugh you out of this entire forest. They're proud of their pure-blooded lineage."

"I know you don't want me to embarrass you. After all, they don't know you too well, and you don't know them that well either. All you have to do is let me show them how tough I am. Hell, we don't have to mention dogs at all. Maybe they'll think I'm just—kinda different."

"I swear you're crazy, Blackeye." He laughed again. "They'll smell the difference. Your howl will be different. Your bark. I'll miss you, little lady. But you're young. You'll get over me. Stay with your own kind. Don't try to be something you ain't."

And that was all he said. I quit licking his dirty sores and started to walk away. I did a proud strut to get as far away from him as fast as I could.

I was about half a mile down the trail when I heard a familiar howl. I would have known it a mile away. That was Super's howl. Was he changing his mind or asserting his leadership over the pack? I had to go back to see. But I walked. Took my time. Looked at the late summer blooms. No way was I going to show that I had forgiven his underestimation of me.

Chapter 36

My body was telling me I was now in full heat, and Super was supercharged to mate.

"Okay, okay, I misspoke," was Super's greeting. "I had forgotten that the main reason I risked all that is handsome about me was because I wanted you more than anything. Will you forgive me for letting everything go to my head, when really what's in my heart is what really counts? Let's get the show on the road."

"But you have other priorities," I reminded him. "Maybe later. I can wait. Don't the humans say that 'true love waits?'"

"I don't want to wait, and I don't think you do either. Let's get it on. The pack is waiting for its virile leader to enlarge its membership."

"No, you're using me, Super. I won't be used."

"And you want to use me," he countered. "What was I hearing from you just minutes ago? I'm making a deal with you, Blackeye. Plus, I know you really want me."

He was right. My female parts were tingling, vibrating with each breath I took. My entire body wanted this wolf so bad. Maybe my body was smarter than my brain. And I knew my heart was oh, so ready.

We hurried through the foreplay. We luxuriated in the scents we both exuded. I licked Super in key areas that would help him perform as the super wolf pack leader he was. And he looked at me with his excited eyes, then licked my rear like he was partaking in a holy meal.

I didn't want to go back to him, but I let my body lead me into pure pleasure. We howled, our voices of deep love and anticipation.

I felt his exuberance, his sheer strength inside me as his front paws embraced my hips. I loved being a wild canine, now mating with the esteemed ancestor species, the wolf. My cubs would be wolfdogs, and I would be extremely proud to be called their mother.

I could feel all of me contracting to embrace every part of Super. Our rears would now stay side by side for half an hour or more as we gloried in our togetherness and playfulness.

All great things must at some time come to an end. But I didn't look at our lovemaking as an ending. No, it was now truly a beginning as our love transitioned into commitment. I hoped I was right this time. At least by now, he knew I meant what I said.

We finally gazed beyond our ecstasy, noticing that we had been the center of attention for the entire pack of elusive wolves.

Would this sharing of our love open their hearts to welcome both Super and me as the alpha male and female? Or would I have to prove myself against another female like Super had done against Almighty?

My eyes spanned the audience, where I noticed a *luna* female who looked like she was ready to defend her status. She bared her teeth and more than hinted that she was ready to take me on. But was I ready for her? I was a lover, not a fighter.

Chapter 37

From sublime ecstasy into the pit of fire. Yes, I was a young bitch, and my thinking worked quickly. It told me I was in trouble. Looking at that luna of the pack, I knew I felt like I was falling into a pit of despair. How could I get out of this fight to the death now facing me with bared teeth?

I ran to Super, who was planning the pack's next hunt with the other hunter wolves. I tapped him on his front paw. "Gotta talk with you for a second," I said. "Just a second, wolves. Important business here."

Super excused himself and joined me by the pile of bones from other hunts. "What's up, babe?" he asked.

"She's after me, that luna from the pack. She's baring her teeth directly my way. I don't know what to do. I can't fight a wolf."

"What do you mean, you can't fight her? A few hours ago, you were bragging about how you were tougher and smarter than every bitch here. Now you say you can't fight this luna?"

I grimaced. "That's kinda right. You should know by now that I'll say anything to have you at my side. I may have overstated just a teeny bit there. What should I do? Can you fight her, or exile her? Maybe you could just declare me the luna, and we'd be done with it."

"Sorry, I can't do that. I faced my music. Now, it's your turn."

"But I'm *with cubs*–your cubs, by the way. Aren't you afraid I might lose them?"

Super laughed. "We mated a few hours ago, and already you're fearful that a fight might make you lose your cubs? Maybe that's why she wants to fight you, to cancel out our mating so she can do the job."

"Don't you dare bark like that. You're no help at all," I complained. "Guess I'll have to use my better sense now that you're alpha. I'll find a way to stall her. Maybe we can negotiate. Shall I share you with her? Would you like that?"

"I gotta get a look at her first," Super said.

I didn't know if he was joking or if he meant that, but that wasn't one of my negotiating options. "Go on back to your meeting. I'll figure out something," I lamented. "Maybe I'll see you later—hopefully alive, but most likely dead."

Rather than walking right over to gossip with the bitches, I took the long way around the den to ponder my problem. I checked my muscles. They were fine, once I found them. My eyesight seemed perfect. I wasn't running into any trees or falling down holes. I seemed to be in perfect shape for a lightweight. But my opponent looked to be a heavyweight. My only solution if she insisted on fighting was to use my brain, which I assumed was superior to hers. After all, dogs evolved from wolves. Thus, we should be smarter.

Then, *she* came again. In other words, the ghost of Mrs. Gregg.

"I see you're scared, little girl. Gotcha some problems? Tell me about them."

"You can't help. It's dog and wolf stuff. You don't fight. So, just go away. I'm thinking."

"Try me," the ghost answered.

"Okay, I'll think out loud, and you can listen. I gotta fight this she-wolf, a luna, in order to keep my mate or even be a member of his pack. Look at me. Do you see a wolf in me? A fighter? A super fighter? Well, this she-wolf didn't get to be a luna by chasing frogs. She's baring her teeth, ready to fight next time she sees me. I'm not ready. I'll never be ready."

"Interesting," Mrs. Gregg said. "I agree. You are puny, even for a dog. But you have your youth and your mate. You use the first to keep the second. I assume she's comfy in her position and won't have the gumption you have. If it's any consolation, invite me to the match. I'll pull some punches of my own, and she'll never know what hit her."

"I don't think I heard you right," I responded. "I get into this fight, but you win it? No, don't go for that. If I gotta fight, then it has to be my fight and not yours."

"Okay, I understand. You're just like that Super Bastard you call your mate. Let me tell you right now, you'll lose big. Your pregnancy will be ended. You're going to be destroyed so badly that you'll be lucky to still be alive, let alone ever mate or carry litters anymore. But at least you'll have your pride. And what good will it do you? Maybe an old, fat bear will put you out of your misery while you wallow in a ditch somewhere."

"Aw, c'mon. I'm not that bad. I'm also fast. I'm much faster than I was when I escaped from your place last year. Sara thought I was pretty great, don't you think?"

"Sara's not in this fight. You are."

I thought by myself for a while. My decision was to invite Mrs. Gregg to a fight, featuring the luna wolf and Blackeye dog. Coming soon, very soon, to the wolf den a few steps away. I was ready, and so was Mrs. Gregg. By this time tomorrow, I would be Queen Blackeye, luna of the pack. Impressive!

Chapter 38

I strutted over to the Divine, the angry luna and her ladies-in-waiting. I glared directly into her rusty eyes. (Beautiful eyes, by the way.) In this instance, however, those very eyes expected me to run away with my tail between my legs. No way.

"I have new cubs being molded in my holy and fertile body right now. Yes, I'm told that I'm not a wolf like the rest of you. But let me assure you that while I have no pedigree, my ancestors are a mixture of courageous breeds. Most likely there are a few wolves in the mix. If so, I'm proud of such a heritage. I've inherited the best of all breeds. See this black spot over my right eye? That's my sign that I won't step back from you now. I'll fight you to the death, if necessary, to defend my cubs as legit members of this pack."

"Good job," Mrs. Gregg whispered in my ear. "Go for the win!"

The luna was tapping her front paw and baring her jagged teeth. She said, "A little on the wordy side, aren't you, bitch? I'm ready to fight. Are you? You don't belong in our pack. Leave now or I'll drag your dead body out of here."

"Just try it. Are you carrying the cubs of the former leader who has now deserted the pack? I'm carrying the cubs of your new alpha. For him, for my descendants, and lastly for me, I am ready to defy your leadership of this pack."

The luna female marched within a paw of my face. She went for my jugular. I moved away from her bite. Her jaw snapped shut in the air.

I immediately tore into her muscular front quarter, thanks to the strength of Mrs. Gregg. We hit a vein and blood shot out into my face. Hurriedly, my paw wiped it away like war paint. The ladies-in-waiting scurried around their leader. She made another attempt, this time to crush my nose, nearly missing it, but nonetheless inflicting intense pain above my bared teeth.

I yelped. But Mrs. Gregg and I were just beginning. This time, I leaped over her and attacked her on her left side, which was vulnerable to my razor-sharp teeth. I bit off a clump of her muscular flesh and spit it into her wide-open mouth. Now, she had two deep cuts from which blood was oozing out all across her front side.

With the encouragement of Mrs. Gregg, I stood my ground. The ladies-in-waiting were huddling around her, trying to aid her as she rapidly lost stamina. I could hear them advising her. One seemed to want to take her place in our match. I changed that lady's mind in no time after one tear over her eye. Then, there was another attack from a third. I nearly tore off her front right paw. Mrs. Gregg was amazingly strong, especially for a dead human.

The deafening howling and growling was now changing to faint yips and yelps. A fourth she-wolf attempted to go for my still-enlarged female parts at my rear. We tore into her side, also drawing blood. By now, my mouth looked like it had been injured. Parts of the other females' skin and fur were dangling from my mouth. I spit it all right back at them. (That I did all by myself.)

I was beginning to think there was a chance, as Mrs. Gregg had assured me, that I could indeed be the victor in this fight. No one made a dive for me. I looked over at Super, who'd just joined the crowd of other spectators. He nodded, then winked, which told me that this was a win for both of us. I had stood my ground. I witnessed those females who had tried to overpower me retreating into the deeper parts of the forest, where they would weep and perhaps plan revenge at a later time. All who remained with me were a few females not involved in the fight, the males, and Mrs. Gregg, floating around somewhere over us. She was the real champ. I looked up and gave her a salute of gratitude. Without her, I wouldn't have stood a chance against such a formidable force.

Nevertheless, to celebrate I howled so the entire forest would hear me. "I am the leader, the alpha, the luna female. I bring with me a new lineage that will embolden this pack of wolves. I am proud to be carrying the cubs this very moment, co-created by your new alpha male, Super. Strong in body and spirit, we will protect and bring respect for the pack from this day forward."

I realized I was taking some of Super's thunder away, so I quieted myself and commenced to lick my own wounds while my mate's chest swelled with pride even more.

As new leadership stepped forward, the male wolves developed a new order of hierarchy within the pack. Super told our worker wolves that they needed to increase the amount of game they would bring back to the pack. He set a timeframe in which the pack would grow in size and strength, and how our territory would grow, and all would be protected and well fed.

And thus began a new era in the life of Super and me. We were no longer a stray and a lone wolf. From the bottom to the top in one day. Long live the alpha male and luna female of the new kingdom. I couldn't wait to see what the future would bring our way, including the addition of other lone wolves who wanted to rejoin the pack. But I also knew there would be enemies who aimed to destroy the entire pack.

Chapter 39

The next couple of months were like a never-ending feast. I grew fatter each day. And no wonder. The other wolves were bringing me delicacies from the forest multiple times a day. I accepted their gifts of deer, turkey, squirrel, rabbit, and other freshly killed critters. The ladies-in-waiting, including even the former luna herself, now called the beta female, groomed me daily. And at night, I slept next to my loving mate, Super.

"Super, is life perfect yet, or should I expect more?" I would sometimes ask Super as I savored my privileged life. He would do his best to remind me that this happiness wouldn't last forever. We had to watch out for unlawful hunters, wild pigs, even nature herself, who could overwhelm us with disease, famine, or catastrophic flooding or forest fires—all of which could challenge our tenuous existence. That was one reason guard wolves were so important in the pack, in front of our cave.

The days continued to get shorter and colder. I could feel the cubs stirring inside me and was sure that this would be a big litter. The wise she-wolf of the pack told me they were now in a birthing position. Any day, labor would start.

And it did. At first, I was quiet and endured alone the tightening of my muscles above my hips in the very back chambers of our cave. Super had gone hunting with his pack of betas and omegas that morning.

A time finally came when my inner moaning turned into outer howls, which summoned the wise she-wolf and her entourage to guide the birth of my cubs. She licked around my birthing canal. She gave me drink from her own saliva and groomed me as I squirmed, paced, and moaned for what seemed like hours.

I had never labored so hard. Regrettably, I had eaten *too much* during my pregnancy. Thus, my cubs were larger than normal, and my body wasn't as limber as it should have been. Instead of a nearly two-year-old, I felt like an old bitch birthing her last litter before retirement.

But nature couldn't be stopped. At last, the firstborn struggled through me into the darkness of the cave. It whimpered. I licked it with love. Then, I felt the second one coming. So far, I had two perfect cubs who would be assets to the pack. And they looked like their father. How I wished Super was with me to experience this miracle, to be among the first to see his cubs.

In all, we produced six wolfdog cubs that day. All were perfect specimens. Three males and three females. I was famished once I knew that all had been birthed. Like their mama, they were hungry, so between the wise she-wolf and me, each was guided to my tits. I could tell by the contented looks on their faces that they loved the taste of me.

Finally, at about twilight, just as snow was beginning to fall, the hunting pack came home. But Super was not among them.

The wise she-wolf came in to tell me the news. The pack had ventured into a field in which sheep were grazing. A shepherd spotted the pack as they were dragging a lamb behind them. Super saw the man with the gun and positioned himself in front of one of his beta males. He was killed with a bullet that went straight into his heart.

I couldn't believe the story. I insisted that I see my lover's body before I would believe it. I rushed through the chambers of the cave to its entrance. The howling among the other wolves was loud enough to wake the entire forest.

For some reason, I thought every other wolf was wrong. "Where is Super?" I howled. "He has his pups waiting for him. Tell him to get home this minute. My cubs need their father."

My ladies-in-waiting rushed to my side. Each she-wolf in her own way tried to tell me that Super was a hero, that he had done what all good alphas did. He had given his life for his pack. I needed to be proud.

I wasn't proud. I wanted to go where he was and to die there with him. I wanted my flesh to decay and mingle with his, to be eaten by the same wild animals that would soon find him.

But then, I awoke to my responsibility. I had new cubs, waiting to feed and raise up, to show the greatness of their father in the months and years ahead.

Chapter 40

My cubs remained perfect copies of their father. One daughter, Stormy, had my black spot on her right eye, but in all the other ways, she also resembled Super. And that was fine with me.

For a while, I wept in deep grief and was inconsolable. Day after day, I expected to see Super enter our cave. He couldn't have been killed. He was too strong for defeat. When I finally accepted that he was dead, anger invaded my soul. How could he have left with the worker wolves on that hunt? Why was the pack invading human pastures and killing their animals while wild game had always been our mainstay for nutrition? Why did he take the bullet to protect one of his omega wolves? He should have stayed with his partner—me—that day.

And I blamed him when it rained all day. I blamed him for a timber rattlesnake coming into our camp. If my day wasn't perfect, it was his fault. Yet at night I longed for his strong embrace. I regretted that his cubs would never see him. Could I still tell them how great their father was, even though I was now bitter? I needed time.

As the alpha female, I also had to rule the pack until another male wolf moved into the leadership role. If you could see me, I was like a dwarf amidst this group of wolves. But I was the Queen Mother in those days. I was responsible for bringing new life and blood into the pack. I knew that there were a few beta females who planned to one day challenge my leadership. And why not? With Super dead, why would I want to stay in this pack? I was prepared to leave without a fight if that was the will of my fellow canines.

Nevertheless, I think I did well during the transition time. After Super's body was returned to the pack, I instructed all pack members to partake of his body. Many balked at the command, so I was the first to bite into his heart so his love would remain with me long after his body had melted into the earth and his spirit had merged into the daily fog that covered our mountains.

I commanded the pack to find us another safer location, deeper in the woods. We needed better access to food, and we needed to be distant from humans' livestock. As it was, I knew that the farmers were out to get us, and that their alphas would give them permission to kill every one of us as threats to agriculture and livestock in the region, even though we were an endangered species. At the very least, they'd load us up and take us to the eastern part of the state. This possibility was about as bad since we loved our mountains here as much as our own lives.

The pack did as they were told. I led my pack with my cubs running beside me as soon as they were mobile. Our betas, omegas, guards, and hunters followed with the she-wolves bringing up the rear. We formed our own little caravan to a more secure, game-plentiful home deeper in the forest. Our home of many caves was replaced by one of many streams. Some wolves refused to move with the pack, and so our size diminished. Sadly, those who refused to relocate were killed within a moon. What days of lamentations our pack endured!

A bright light during these moons of mourning was the growth of my dear cubs. Even I had trouble telling them apart, other than Stormy, the female with the black spot. Eventually the cubs developed personalities which helped me distinguish them. I could tell that there were two alpha males and two alpha females. The alpha males were Fury and Righteous. The alpha females were Stormy and Star. My one male and female who seemed to be betas, or helpers, were Ready and Mercy.

I loved them all. I was immensely gratified that my bloodline as a dog was pumping through these wolfdogs, as well as Super's red wolf blood.

I started weaning my cubs after about two moons. They took the hint and started following me out of my cave. We would galivant in the woods, creating quite a sight for the other animals around us. Some of these other small animals like mice, voles, moles, and some squirrels by now were easy for me to kill. Even though Old Pat and I loved eating dumpster food, he also encouraged me to eat wild food. "You'll never be a true wild animal until you let the wild feed you," he would often say.

Plus, my cubs did better on tiny wildlife as starters. Baby critters were easier to catch and much easier to digest. In the early stages, they would watch me catch an opossum, for example. Then, I would chew up the most tender muscle and fat, spitting them out so my cubs could learn how to eat fresh, wild food. At first, most of them turned their noses up at my chewed-up food. Stormy and Fury were the exceptions. There wasn't anything they wouldn't pick up in their mouths and try to chew on. The other four finally copied them when they got hungry enough. Soon, they too hungered for "fresh flesh," as I called it.

As far as the big game went—like deer, bear, and wild pigs—I left the training for killing them to our hunting parties, which fascinated my younguns as they got old enough to stay with the hunter wolves.

Within six months, I was almost done with all this smothering mothering. I took them to a rendezvous site and wandered off—always aware of where they were, however. By the time they were eight months old, they blended in with the rest of the pack. I knew that once I had given them their independence, I would again come into season. I was in no rush to get to that point.

But nature has her way. Within ten months after I'd given birth to my wolf pups, I could feel my body going through the signs that would put me into heat. I knew that would bring a few strong lone wolves to our den, one of which I would choose to mate with.

Most red wolf packs, which are at risk of extinction, are led by an alpha male and female. In my case, after Super died, I became the only alpha (or luna) in the pack, and it remained that way until I came into heat again, about ten months later. When a female wolf goes into heat, her scent attracts male wolves who are loners, like Super was, and other wolves already in the pack who think they can take on the role. Since we were the only pack left in this mountainous part of the state, I wouldn't meet any wolves from other packs. The new competing alphas in all cases couldn't be related to me. We knew that incest wouldn't benefit the pack.

My ladies-in-waiting could smell the tell-tale signs first. Then, the males took notice. They knew I didn't care to mate with them, so they kept their distance. A few ventured to get closer, but a good growl and bared teeth usually sent my message to get away.

As I got closer to my most fertile time, a few new males showed up to court me. They all looked to be wolves. I wanted the strength that came with wolf parentage for my next litter. I narrowed my choices down to two strong dudes.

One, who called himself Skyhawk, was tolerable to me. He lacked the pride and humor of Super, but he had the body traits I found attractive and would carry over well into my new litter of cubs. The other candidate was Grandeur, who was built of iron and was proud of it.

We needed to get this show on the road. I reminded both that they would have to earn my loyalty by asserting themselves as the alpha of the pack. Since none of the males currently in the pack were alpha material, they would have to fight each other until one gave up or was killed.

They both were strong and ferocious males. Both were youngish and would probably use their fresh wisdom to secure abundant food and safety for the pack. I wasn't attracted to Grandeur, but for the pack's sake, I would mate with the winner of their battle of superiority, which would begin at dawn the next day.

I took the best spot in the den, where the three streams met. Grandeur started the battle, by wasting no time. With his distinct howl signifying his virility, he bared his teeth and rushed into Skyhawk, tearing at his flesh until his opponent's blood covered his face. Skyhawk yelped and tried to strike back. He aimed for the chest of Grandeur but missed his mark because Grandeur turned completely around, confusing Skyhawk. Grandeur tore again into the same wound he had bloodied just seconds earlier.

Skyhawk knew he was no competition for Grandeur. Not ready to fight to the death, he backed away and ran off, meaning I would mate with Grandeur and a new era would begin for our pack.

I congratulated the winner and gestured to him that I was ready to mate with him tomorrow morning, if my body was ripe for the encounter. After smelling him and licking his rear, I vanished into my den and tried to reassure myself that as the alpha female, it was my duty to submit to the strongest male and the leader of the pack. My wise she-wolf joined me in my cave.

Together, we checked my body in preparation for the mating ordeal. The excitement was gone. Grandeur was no Super; not even a Skyhawk.

"If you want, you can leave now," my old she-wolf suggested. "I don't think you will find Grandeur to be the perfect partner you were hoping for."

She knew I agreed, but Skyhawk had run off in disgrace. I knew the rules of the pack, so I said, "Oh, no, I will stay. I have a responsibility to—"

We both heard gunshots coming from outside the den. As we emerged from the cave entrance, we saw two dying wolves who had been guarding my quarters. More shots burst into the den, and two more wolves fell to the ground.

"Go, go now!" the wise she-wolf yelped as she pushed me out of the den. "Now, run like the deer!"

This was my chance. I looked back once and then ran as far as my legs would carry me. I didn't have the slightest idea what would happen to my sons and daughters.

Chapter 41

Gunshots continued to explode through the air. When I was out of range, guilt began to fill my heart. I was alone. I had left all six of my cubs behind. How could I have deserted my pups? I had to go back. If Super could give his life for a worker wolf, I had to give my life for my cubs.

There was a lull in the shooting for a few minutes as I stealthily made my way back to the den. Along the way, even before I set foot into our den, I saw three of my beautiful cubs dead on the ground. They were all within paw-lengths of each other. So innocent. They had not an evil bone in their bodies. Yet they were indiscriminately gunned down because of who they would grow up to be. Bodies from my body. Why? Why? So many of my cubs had not had a chance to carry on the wolf family line. Star, Ready, and Mercy were bleeding into the dust, blood forming a dark puddle around them. Streams of blood would eventually form a bigger stream before merging into the river of life in the valley. I inhaled their unique scents and licked and kissed each while my entire insides were boiling. I hoped to hear a beating heart or feel a breath. My hopes were dashed. There was no life left in their fragile bodies.

From one of the bushes off to the side, I could feel eyes peeking over at me. My fighting instincts raged through my body. I bared my teeth and growled in the direction of the bushes. Humans were soon to become endangered now that this luna was avenging her dead cubs. But no human had the guts to get close to our den. They had fired from a safe distance.

In the midst of my sorrow, I saw six eyes peering into mine. Blinking and traumatized, these eyes belonged to my three remaining offspring: Fury, Stormy, and Righteous. I could feel milk gathering in my tits, even though, by now, the cubs had been weaned for months.

I had to leave my three dead cubs bathing in their own blood and reunite with my living cubs. I was grieving, but also rejoicing. All in all, my relief in finding some of my cubs alive won out.

"Let's get out of here," I commanded. "We must flee now, go as far as we can. We'll hide for a few days where they'll never find us. From there, we'll discuss our plans for the rest of our lives."

My living cubs, although appearing to be full-grown wolfdogs, still lacked the maturity to make their own decisions. They needed an alpha mother to groom and teach them the dangers of the world outside the pack and the den. That world had once given them a sense of safety and strength. But no more. Outsiders had now invaded our den itself. Where could we hide?

We ran as fast as we could, east into the forest. We passed more dead wolves, including Grandeur himself. For those still alive in the pack, I was sorry I didn't call out to them to follow me. But my cubs and my mother-hood came before leading a pack. I grieved that their new leader was now dead. But for me personally, I felt relieved that he would never mate with me.

All I could do was howl. They knew my howl. They knew my scent. They would find me and follow. I told the cubs to keep running and not look back.

Stormy was the first to tire. "Mama, I can't go any farther," she yelped. "We've passed thousands of trees."

I could see that even Fury's and Righteous's coats were soaking wet. Their tongues were hanging from their mouths as they panted incessantly.

"Let's just go as far as that stream over there, where we can drink and rest below the bank. But for just only a little while, mind you. It will be dark soon. We have to find a hideout for the night far away from that blood-soaked land and its murderers."

The three of them jumped into the water to cool down, even though the weather was getting colder, and the wind was picking up.

"Out of there now. We don't need you all getting sick while on the run," I insisted, as my senses told me that we weren't out of danger yet.

Like the respectful cubs they had been trained to be, they were back with me within a few breaths. We were then on our way again, but this time at a somewhat slower pace.

We came to a series of gigantic rocks where a timber road dipped behind them. By now, I had learned that where rocks rose above the ground, there were caves nearby. We each surveyed the area in all four directions. As the sun dissolved into the horizon, Fury barked in jubilation. "Up here, Mama."

The other two cubs yelped, and I shushed, telling them to keep their mouths shut for a little longer until we could bark quietly. We were at Fury's side as fast as we could run. He led us into a deep, hollowed-out cave that was hidden behind a grove of young trees.

"Perfect," I praised my son. "Your father would be so proud of you, as I sure am."

We were too tired to eat that night. We had lots of plans to work out. And by now, I was extremely fertile and uncomfortable. My male pups knew better, from nature herself, to not to fool with me, for which I was grateful. However, I needed to find the right male soon amidst all this other confusion. I moved to the very end of the cave where I would be hidden from the males who would be coming a-courtin'.

Through the night, we argued about where our next home should be. The pups wanted to stay where we were. Fury, being the alpha male, was proud of this place he had found.

"I say, let's stay here. Tomorrow, we will hunt some food nearby and rest up."

"We can fix this up real nice, Mama," said Stormy. "Plus, you know what? You're in season. You need to mate soon. With so many slaughtered wolves today, we all need to think and do our part to build up another pack."

I wondered if her words meant that soon she, herself, would have to deal with coming into season. I couldn't believe how my little she-wolf had matured so fast. But by her age, I'd already birthed my first litter.

With those thoughts in mind, I dozed off for the night. The only things disturbing us were bats coming back into the cave and the awful odors they left in our new home. A den cleaning would need to be scheduled as soon as possible. The bats would have to find a new home, no question about it.

Chapter 42

The next morning brought us sunshine and a soft breeze. I was the first to emerge from our cave. And there before me were suitors. Among them was Skyhawk, who was putting on a strut as though the licking he took yesterday was merely a bad dream.

I looked over other suitors, some of whom were dogs like me, who were willing to fight to the death to be my mate. Of course, none, not even Skyhawk, could ever fill the void that Super had left in my heart. He had been my first love and would always be a sweet nugget of delight in my memory.

"Okay, you wolves and dogs, I'm only mating with one of you, and this time that wolf will be Skyhawk," I said. "He had attempted to lead our pack, which was demolished by humans yesterday. He is the alpha male to lead this new pack that I and my children are forming now. We do need betas and omegas to be our workers. You can join our pack if these are positions you want to fill." I was proud of my budding assertive leadership at that moment.

Skyhawk bowed down before me as some of the other wolves wandered away. A few took up my offer to join the pack, which made me hopeful. I winked at Skyhawk, and toward him I walked my swollen, tired body, oozing with burning hormones that begged for a male's strong embrace.

Foreplay began the mating dance initially. I needed to get used to his scent, to taste his sweat and saliva. We both needed to kiss one another's rears before I would walk backwards into his caressing mount.

Aww, he felt so good to my tired body. This mating experience was beginning to open me up physically and symbolically. Skyhawk was gentle and powerful. Between howls and lingering smells from opened pores, I thought this guy might be a perfect alpha, if only to make my body come alive. I could manage the other wolves. Already we were molding into a familiarity with each other. I was the bitch he had lost a fight for, and he had the strength my body wanted to lean into.

And all that was just the foreplay. As we moved into the second movement of this sensuous dance, I was experiencing nothing but pure pleasure in my spirit, in my nerves—in my entire body. Skyhawk was a gift without the ego of Super. I wanted to let him wrap his body around mine, and then to explore all I had inside me. I wanted to have his cubs. I wanted to snuggle with him tonight and every night. Sheer ecstasy made me his.

We savored this adventure as his body filled mine, not only with his seed for the future of our pack, but with hope and knowledge that nothing would be able to extinguish our love. It was like we were tied in a knot and time was standing still, simply for us.

Suddenly, we heard spectators in the pack cheering us as my body released his. We howled in unison for ourselves and for all those who trusted our leadership as we forged ahead in expectation.

Chapter 43

My new partner, Skyhawk, and I retired into my cave. I discovered that he too had some dog in him, but he still carried the major traits of wolves—the brownish coat with streaks of black and white, the prominent ears always at attention, and rusty-colored eyes.

"I respect your canine bloodline," Skyhawk told me. "At first, I didn't want to dilute my lineage even more by mating with a dog. But the chemistry, your alpha mannerisms, evidence of a strong genetic line, and nurturing abilities I'd heard about with your previous litter—all these convinced me that you were the bitch for me."

"And I wasn't particularly drawn to you either, Skyhawk," I confessed. "Yet I noticed that you would be a gentle partner and respect my desires. I think we'll make a great partnership here. I will need you so much as the new cubs grow in my belly. Whenever I feel life in me, I will now think of you."

Fury, Stormy, and Righteous listened to our vows to care for each other in the upcoming months. I heard a few moans outside the cave entrance. Stormy and Fury were probably mimicking our conversation. I loved my cubs' sense of humor.

"I will honor you as our new alpha leader," I told Skyhawk. "But I'm worried, very worried. I don't think we're safe here or maybe anywhere. We need to come up with plans to save our small pack. I don't want to be alone in the world outside of my pack. We don't stand a chance as lone wolves—or dogs—out there."

"Agreed. Although I lost the battle to lead the former pack, I know this is my second chance," Skyhawk added. "With your help, we will guard you with the help of your older cubs as we prepare for the new ones we'll later gather around us. I really believe we will grow and once again rule this old growth forest, forgotten by humans, but inviting to us. We will hunt and consume wild game only. Humans will think we've been destroyed and forget about us as time goes on. For now, however, we have cause for celebration, but one that is quiet. Our pack is reborn today in the spirit of the wild, while in your sacred body new members are forming at this moment. Let us feast and cautiously repeat our promises to the pack."

I was impressed with this positive and philosophical alpha. "So, send out our hunters two by two into the woods. Find a deer we can feast on tonight."

Skyhawk called his finest hunters, betas and omegas, who had escaped the slaughter yesterday, and they promptly started their hunt. The partying would make this a late night, since the sun had already sunk beneath the ground. In the meantime, I would settle down with my new family—my three cubs and our new pack leader, Skyhawk.

But the party was not to happen. Once more, humans would intervene, as they loved to do in this world that they thought was theirs alone to rule.

Chapter 44

A different sort of hunting group invaded our small pack. We couldn't even celebrate our new alliance of a newborn pack made from remnants of the old and former lone wolves.

These hunters carried strange-looking guns. They spoke quietly and methodically with no emotions. Each had a different job. How they had evaded being apprehended before they got to our den, I didn't know. They encircled our small outpost and started shooting. There was very little sound like the guns we'd heard yesterday. These were more like arrows being aimed at us from guns. I saw my cubs go down upon impact from the pellets on the tips of the arrows. Then, Skyhawk and I were struck, and that was it. It was as though we'd entered another world, still alive but momentarily dead.

Next thing I knew, I was in what humans might call a laboratory. Everything was sickeningly clean. Smells of unpleasant chemicals permeated the big room. We were each put on one of those gray, slick, gleaming tables, where we were poked with needles, and our mouths were explored with long, silver instruments that showed reflections of whatever they were looking at on the end, a little like the window Mrs. Gregg had used when she decorated her face. The humans invaded my private parts, as well as Skyhawk's, and even my cubs' private parts. They carried around little black tablets that younger humans were clicking as the older ones dictated to them.

The den, the forest, the pack—they were all gone. We were all stuck outside of the wild now. As my pups seemed to come out of their stupor, they became frantic, especially Fury and Stormy. I wanted to get up and tend to them, to shelter them near my chest. I had never told them about the dangers of being in the human world.

The humans finally seemed to get all the information they were looking for. Like at the shelter, we were each put into cages with dry dog food and water infused with stinking chemicals. My pups threw up. I didn't eat or drink any of this human poison.

After the scientists had left for the night, I barked to my pups about what I thought was going on. These people wanted to learn about us, so they got into our bodies and explored every little part of us. I told them that I didn't think they would kill us. Instead, they would observe us until they got tired of us. We should make life unpleasant for them, so they would eventually return us to where they found us.

Skyhawk listened in. He had some concept of what was happening. After all, I had called him philosophical.

"Okay, y'all. Let's call it a night," he ordered like a true alpha. "No deer, but our pack members will feast without us and howl out our names. They won't forget us, and one day we'll join them again. In the meantime, don't cooperate with the enemy."

I was proud of my partner. Even I went to sleep and dreamed of my new cubs being created in my body. I would do all I could to see that they entered this life out in the wild where they belonged.

Chapter 45

The next day, the scientists were back. They took us from our cages and did more explorations of our bodies. They talked about me especially, since I appeared to be a dog. They assumed that I had mated with Skyhawk, and that the smaller animals were wolfdogs, probably an earlier litter that Skyhawk and I had created.

I wanted to howl out Super's name, to tell them how Righteous and Fury were almost exact copies of their father. But I realized it wouldn't matter to them.

When all the exams—the touching and poking, stretching and squeezing—were done, they tranquilized us again, this time with strong liquids they inserted into our thighs that would put us into a death-like deep sleep.

When we started to wake, I could see that we were being transferred to smaller vehicles, which could traverse the rocky and forest-covered terrain, and eventually stop at the place where they had found us.

All of my cubs and Skyhawk were released, except for me. At the last minute, the bossman seemed to tell the others not to release me. He would take me home with him. He liked me and my strong will. There was more to learn from me.

I was shocked and outraged. Skyhawk and my cubs were howling and had formed a circle clawing at the tough vehicle I was still caged in. Baring my teeth and growling at my new human owner did no good.

All of this made him want to take me home even more. Seeing that my noncooperation wasn't working, I put my head between my paws and cried my eyes out.

Chapter 46

So here I am, curling up on a nice little cushion in a human's perfect house. The owner, Master Tom, has a woman in his life, pregnant just like me. But she's with her lover. I am far away from mine and may never see him again.

I've heard them talking. They don't know that I can understand every word they say. Tom wants to abort my cubs. He doesn't think I can birth them from a mate who is so much larger than I am. Can't he see that I've already had litters with both another wolf and a bigger dog? I've gotta somehow convince him that his idea won't fly with me. Maybe his wife being pregnant will sway him to save my pups.

Every day, I stand by the door looking for a chance to escape from this smothering house with its bright lights, hardwood floors, and Alexa being commanded to provide information, which she provides with never a mean word from a funny little box. Mrs. Gregg comes to me engulfed in a mysterious cloud, while a round box is where Alexa seems to live.

Yes, I've had to wear that collar again, but this one is considerably larger. Tom has taken me downtown to show me off. I get so sick of humans coming up to me and shedding their germs on me as they attempt to pet me. I usually growl and groan. Tom gets embarrassed, but I don't care. The sooner I can get out of here, the better.

I constantly think of my cubs and Skyhawk, even Super, Old Pat, and Mrs. Gregg. So far, only Mrs. Gregg comes to me in that cloud she likes to wrap herself in. Her advice: *Stay alert. Never give up*. And do all I can to protect the developing litter in my belly. My cubs will never forget their mother—me—just as I've never forgotten mine.

One thing I envy about humans is that they can communicate with others far away. They type messages called emails, or they pick up their little flat devices and call other humans. If I could only talk to my lost pups and Skyhawk. But even better, if I could only smell and lick them, curl up in a big ball with them during these cold months now upon us.

Tom is one of these humans who work for Uncle Sam, who he calls his boss. It may be a nickname. But he likes to do everything perfect. He likes his life to run like a clock, to have his house orderly (poor Heather, his wife). He doesn't eat meat and would like Heather not to, either. If she could understand my barks, she would know that I think she needs to eat meat now for her baby inside her. Maybe seeing me gobble up lots of meat from the can sends the right message.

Tom's next project, other than work, is to send me to obedience school so I will be his perfect pet.

I tell him no way, but he can't seem to understand my barks, growls, and howls like dogs do. Anyway, I'll be going away for a few weeks soon to learn how to "serve" Master Tom as a nice and obedient mid-sized dog and become his "best friend."

Chapter 47

The training people accepted me into their program. At first, their kindness toward me was overdone. Maybe they wanted to bond with me, but I knew what they were up to. I told them in so many barks that they were wasting their time. All I wanted was to be released so I could find my pack in time to deliver my litter. I needed Skyhawk and the wise she-wolf at my side. Would these humans want to be around only dogs when they were having *their* one or two babies? Of course, they didn't understand a word I barked.

They assigned one male human named Howard to me. He wanted me to learn commands, like *sit*, *stay*, *fetch*, and especially *no*. Easy enough, but I wasn't about to play their games, like catching their balls or running around in circles. They treated me like a robot and expected me to be thrilled whenever they slipped me a treat. The stuff made me think they were trying to get me hooked on manufactured dog candy, and it didn't even taste decent.

After about ten sunrises and sunsets, I realized I had to pretend I'd learned my training and needed to go back to Master Tom's house. In one day, I passed in flying colors, swallowing lots of icky treats. I was now ready for Tom to pick me up with my pretty certificate saying that I am now obedient, polite, and non-threatening to anybody. Me? An alpha dog? Never threatening? They should see me around squirrels and trout.

Master Tom put me in the front seat of his car for the ride back to his place. He talked to me incessantly as he maneuvered his way through traffic. He called me Madie, by the way.

"So, Madie, I'm so proud of how you were able to do so well in dog training. I'm sure we'll be best friends now. You know, don't you, that you're not a wolf? You're a dog. You need a master like me, and sometimes Heather. We need someone we can trust around our baby when she comes. In the meantime, we need to stop and see the vet so you can be fixed."

My ears went into alert mode when he talked about the stop he'd planned to make at the vet's, who would take care of "my condition" and would fix me so I'd never get in that "condition" again.

Did I really just hear that?

That's when all the dog training in the world disappeared. I gave so-called Master Tom the dirtiest look I could muster, mixed in with droplets of tears from my adorable puppy dog eyes.

No, absolutely not! These pups were mine, Skyhawk's, and most of all, our pack's.

They were not his. He wouldn't kill his own baby, would he? How I wished I could get him to understand that dogs, wolves, probably all animals had instincts, including love. We were all creatures who wanted our genes to continue, to merge with a mate's genes, to make our small pack stronger and better. These cubs in me now, wiggling around inside me, wanted that opportunity. And if he disagreed and attempted to destroy them like Mr. Winter cruelly ended Leader's life, all the training in the world wouldn't prevent me from going after Tom's jugular vein any moment now.

Whew! Good thing he hadn't heard what I was thinking and howling about. But he had to know I wasn't pleased.

I tried to look pleadingly into his eyes, but most of his attention was on the road ahead. So, I continued my howling, mixed in with a few attention-getting tough barks and sad begging yips.

He finally pulled off the road. I didn't know if he would lecture me or try to sympathize. Knowing Tom, I thought about how I would respond to his lecture.

He would remind me that he and Heather loved me. Their baby would, too. In no time at all, I would forget about these cubs I was now carrying. Dogs didn't love the way humans did. The world already had too many hungry dogs. Hadn't I seen the advertisements on TV yet? And lastly, he would say to sit up straight and stop complaining. As a human, he knew what was best for me.

And that would probably be the condensed version. I had answers to all of his points, because I was smart and a fast thinker.

I would tell him that the red wolves were almost extinct. Yes, I was a dog, but my descendants would be almost pure red wolves. I knew love from the times I suckled from my loving mama's tits to the births of two litters already. I felt love when Leader was mercilessly killed by a farmer because he was part wolf, when half of my own recent litter was gunned down by hunters, and now I felt love during this separation from the remainder of that litter. I heard their howls for me nightly, especially when the moon was full. He had no right to tell me that I didn't know what love was. Then, there was my love for Old Pat, whose life I saved from a needle of poison at the humane shelter. He was able to die while free and in nature. And there was Super, who took a bullet for a member of the pack. I would cry. Humans couldn't stand a female's tears.

But I didn't get that lecture. Tom turned and looked into my eyes. He smiled and scratched behind my ears. "I love you so much, my Madie. You and I are going to be best friends."

That was it. He started the car again and focused on his driving.

So, naturally, I focused on complaining. Didn't he see that his best friend was hurting? I needed my family and my pack. They needed me. I needed my den to birth my cubs. I started barking and howling. I tried to poke my head out of the window on the passenger's side. I scratched at the window, thinking if I clawed it hard enough, I could break it or at least get it to lower so I could jump out.

This time, Tom yelled. "Stop that right now! You know better. We're going to the vet, and we're going to fix you. There's nothing you can do about it."

I moved to the floor below my seat and wept, moaning the coming deaths of my darling cubs. I had done all I could do. I glanced mournfully over at Tom.

He was crying, too. Once again, he stopped the car, this time by a hiking trail in the woods. "Will you ever accept me, little girl? Have you been wild too long? I'll be patient. You'll get the best food in the world. I'll allow you to meet up with other dogs and wrestle with 'em. We'll arrange grooming. Maybe, just maybe we'll—we'll—okay, I'll say it—let you have your pups."

At first, I wanted to plaster his freshly shaved face with licks and kisses. Then, I realized he'd not mentioned my weaned cubs, my mate Skyhawk, or the pack.

I shook my head no.

"What do you want, Madie?" he shouted.

I was silent.

"Well, that's just too bad. I don't care anymore. You're just a dog with no sense."

Tears ran down my face as he started the car again, let a car whiz by him, and inched into the road. I could see that he was frustrated. He had tried to reason with what he assumed was a dumb dog in need of being fixed. He probably thought he was losing it.

This time, he pulled off the road one more time, not far from the trail. He attached the leash to my collar, helped me out of the car on the passenger side, and said, "Let's go for a walk."

He led the way onto the trail while he talked to himself. He had given up trying to reason with me. All I heard was, "Maybe I should—" or "But it doesn't make sense—" and "What if—?"

I sat down smack in the middle of the trail. As I was trying to tune out Tom's utterances, I wondered what was beyond that hill ahead of us. Then, he turned around, took a few steps back, and sat down next to me. I could tell he was tired, too.

"Okay, Madie. I'm done with thinking I can change or make a better world for you. I'm going against everything I've been taught about pets and dogs—you know, stuff like that. I love animals. We humans want to care for you. But I guess there are some of you who desire freedom more than anything. Am I right?"

I nodded my pointed nose up and down. Our eyes met. Mine were full of tears. Now, like a silly human, he was hugging me. I think if he had been a dog, he would have been licking and drooling all over me. He unbuckled my collar, stood up, and said, "You can go now."

He just stood there. He made a gesture with his arm. I got the message. Even if I got the message wrong, this was my chance.

I took off up the trail, running as fast as my doggie legs would carry me. I briefly stopped and looked back.

There was Tom, still standing where he'd freed me, but now, he was waving goodbye. "And don't you dare tell any humans that I did this, you hear?" he shouted.

I bowed one more time to a human. To me, he had discovered what true perfection was.

I didn't know how I would do it, but I would find my cubs and Skyhawk tonight. Maybe Mrs. Gregg would guide me.

Don't get me wrong. I still don't like humans, but there are a few out there that aren't too bad. They realize that sometimes being a best friend is being willing to let go.

Discussion Questions

1. Why do you think Blackeye wanted to be wild?

2. Have you ever desired freedom like Blackeye or Mrs. Gregg did?

3. What do you think of Blackeye's opposition to being fixed?

4. Explain your feelings regarding Blackeye's abandonment of her only living pup at the Winters' home.

5. Do you think animals think and feel a little, or a lot, like humans do?

6. How does Blackeye manipulate humans and other animals she comes into contact with?

7. Can you predict what the rest of Blackeye's life will be like? Do you think she'll eventually move back to live with humans?

8. Explain what a meeting with her mother would be like. How about Sara, of the pups left behind?

9. Do you think it's possible for a pack of wolves to live secretly in the N.C. mountains today?

10. Is this a book that women can relate to, especially concerning gender and male-female relationships?

11. What do you think of Blackeye's friendship with Old Pat?

12. Why do you think the scientists were interested in Blackeye's family?

13. Did Master Tom do the right or wrong thing when he released Blackeye?

14. Did it bother you that Blackeye could tell her story in her own words?

15. Do you think animals, both females and males, enjoy sex like humans do?

Acknowledgments

First, I want to thank all the pet owners who have entered and left my life from the time I was a child to my advanced adult life. One thing I've noticed in recent years is how dogs now are members of the family, as opposed to fulfilling roles such as guardian and herder. Today, I thank the passionate dog lovers and advocates who have dedicated their lives to improving the lives of their dogs and assisting new dog owners on bringing up puppies, and even letting go at the end of your best friend's life.

One author who gave me a peek into a dog's life was Jack London, who wrote *The Call of the Wild*. My book also looks at the lives of wolves, ancestors of the modern dog, and even an alley cat. One resource I found was Nancy Kay LaPorta, who started Full Moon Farm Wolfdog Sanctuary in Black Mountain, North Carolina. I regret that I didn't find out about her sanctuary until after I had submitted my manuscript. She still lives in Western North Carolina but has recently closed her nonprofit facility. I hope she can educate me more, even after this book is published.

I want to thank all my family, friends, and neighbors who have let me spend nearly thirty days in solitude as I struggled to write nearly two thousand words a day toward my more than fifty-thousand-word novel.

Once again, I can't be thankful enough for the expert advice and corrections from my detail-minded editor, Mindi Friedwald, an author herself. She helped me flesh out scenes that needed more depth. In addition, I can't forget my publisher, Janie Jessee, of Jan-Carol Publishing, Inc., from nearby Johnson City, Tennessee, and Draco Bailey, her Communications Director. Their patience in working with this aging, first-time novel writer has given me hope in our sometimes-crazy world.

More appreciation goes out to my next-door neighbor and dog-lover, Autumn Squirrell, who looked over part of my manuscript before it was handed to my editor.

Lastly, a never-ending thank you to my five children and eight grandchildren, who have always been just a phone call, or a few miles drive, away— always accessible to encourage me on the long road that finally reaches publication. Blessings to all of you. Particular thanks go out to Scout, my only granddog. He's a lively and loving mixed German Shepherd, not a sidewalk dog himself, but a friend who also likes the wide-open wild spaces near the Pisgah National Forest behind his home.

About the Author

Rachael Roberts Bliss grew up on a traditional farm and went to church every Sunday and Holy Day at St. Patrick's Catholic Church in Dunlap, Iowa. She knew she wanted to be a writer when she saw tears in her father's eyes as he read her last school newspaper editorial in *The Dunlap Reporter*.

During those middle years between book learning at Estherville Junior College (now a part of Iowa Lakes Community College) and The University of Iowa and retirement nearly fifty years later, Bliss helped create and raise five children and worked in television and print media, but found more fulfillment working for social justice nonprofits that focused on hunger, the environment, poverty, peace, and justice. Her last job was as an AmeriCorps VISTA volunteer in her sixties.

Now living in Asheville, North Carolina, Bliss has taken courses in photography and writing at Asheville-Buncombe Tech Community College and The University of North Carolina-Asheville's Great Smokies Writing Program. When she's not pecking away on her laptop, she's playing grandma with her eight grandchildren or demonstrating for peace and justice at home and throughout the world.

Bliss has authored previous books, including an e-book written under her pen name, Bliss Millard, *Quest for Loves Lost*, available through Smashwords.com, and two paperback print books, *The Goddess of Promised Land: Genesis (Book One)* and *The Goddess of Promised Land: Lamentations (Book Two)*, available through this publisher, locally, and online.

You can keep up with her ups and downs on:

⊕ GoddessofPromisedLand.com

𝐟 Rachaelrobertsbliss

𝕏 PeoplePowerGran

◉ Goddessofpromisedland

www.ingramcontent.com/pod-product-compliance
Lightning Source LLC
Chambersburg PA
CBHW030254270626
47156CB00022B/2759